SILVER DUST

MIST RIDERS
BOOK THREE

Stella Fitzsimons

BUTTERFLY ELECTRIC PRESS

For Dylan,
the greatest storyteller in my life

SILVER DUST

The Chronicles of Luna Mae

Chapter 1

THE CAB DROPPED ME at the gate of the Bella Rosa apartment complex. I stalled at the curb for a moment, clutching onto my stuffed green suitcase. San Diego felt different somehow, cheerless, less inviting, as if I was no longer welcome.

I inhaled and considered calling another cab back to the airport and a return flight to Stockholm. Part of me never wanted to leave Europe, but Grandma sounded excited on the phone when I mentioned possibly coming home for Easter break, and Celia promised to arrange a meeting with her secret liaison, the super-skilled seer who supposedly could look into my past far more effectively than Celia herself.

I was able to come back to my San Diego apartment because of Winter's generosity. He had paid off my lease for a full year. He was like a toothache. No matter what I did, it was impossible to rid him from my thoughts. He lingered like an earworm of some catchy tune I'd much rather forget.

With a sigh, I hauled my luggage on its spinner wheels through the gate. Two boys on electric scooters zipped past. I stumbled backwards and watched them dart down the sidewalk, perilously swerving around each other, shouting and laughing like the world was their private playground.

My elemental magic reacted to a disturbance—one of the scooters bumped into something and careened toward the street. The boy panicked, losing control. I engulfed him in a transparent magnetic field that leapt from my hands of its own accord, gently nudging the scooter back onto the sidewalk and away from oncoming traffic.

The second boy stared at his friend, astonished. Neither boy was entirely sure what they had just witnessed. A moment later, they shrugged it off and sped away on their scooters.

My command of magic grew more nuanced and effective every day. Sometimes it felt like instinct more than choice. When it came out smooth like that, I no longer felt the usual sizzles and reverberations.

I climbed the stairs to my apartment, dragging my suitcase behind me. I wasn't naïve. I knew that Winter had people on me, and I was certain that by now he would know I was back in San Diego. Sooner or later he would reach out and I'd have to sit through a full-blown lecture. I was already working on ways I could shut him up. Looking back, I had started to believe he could sense my etheric essence from a distance, and I wouldn't put it past him to have wiretapped my landline. I was ready for anything and expected the worst, yet, to find him sitting on my couch, broad-shouldered, in a tight workout shirt and shorts, caught me off guard. The allure of his defined musculature made it annoyingly hard not to stare.

He was leafing through one of my history books—well, maybe it was his book now, considering he had bought it, like most of the books on my shelves, after the soul swallowers pulverized the original volumes.

Winter arched an eyebrow. "You seem surprised. Scandinavia has clearly dulled your senses."

I was conscious of the fact that I was scowling at him. I built a fake little smile to help fight off a few choice words. My senses were fine, I had just learned to shut them off and prioritize other things, *important things.*

"Oh, Winter, why don't you make yourself at home?" I said.

His face lit up like my sarcasm was just what the doctor ordered. "Don't be cross. I'm just making sure you're alright."

"I'm alright. Goodbye."

A crease formed between his eyebrows. "You need to let bygones be bygones, Luna Mae."

"Do I? Okay. *Bye. Be gone.*"

"You want me gone, at least until you screw up as you certainly will do. And then it will be, *Where's Jonas gone off to? Oh, how could I use his help?* And then I'll come back and slip on my rubber gloves and busy myself with the task of cleaning up yet another mess."

I threw my hands up in the air. "You live in your own fucked-up reality, you know that? There's no mess here, unless you count all the delusions of grandeur spilling out of your mouth."

"No mess? Really? And yet you're putting yourself into lethal danger."

For the love of God.

"Really, Winter? It's spring break. I'm not in danger. Gram wanted to spend Easter with me. End of story."

He shook his head. "The story never ends. The moment you returned without telling me, you put us both in danger."

Drama much? Sheesh.

"So, now you know," I said. "Crisis averted."

"If only Chaos and Horror were crises that could be easily managed," he said with a deep sigh. "I'm using everything in my power to keep you shielded. The least you could do is let me know when you change continents."

I shrugged. "We're doing this, huh? We're just going to pretend you're not having me watched... dude, you knew full well I was coming home."

He furrowed his brow. "Stunts like this leave me no choice. You're not taking any of this seriously."

"Oh, but I do, trust me. When every single move I make is monitored by your Immortal pals in Stockholm, I need to be seriously seductive when I change my underwear or take a shower or make love. You know, give the boys a show. They work hard."

My words had the desired effect. His features contorted despite his colossal effort to show no emotion whatsoever. "You're joking. Obviously."

I chuckled. "I wouldn't be so sure, Mister Methuselah. Do you think any of your men would have the courage to tell you about my lovers?"

Plural. Good job, Luna. Why pull punches, right?

He kept staring at me, not quite sure I was bluffing.

"I mean, they know, they're perceptive."

"Know what?" he said.

I smiled. "They know you expected the naïve witchling to fall head over heels for you and just sit in her room, pining away for your return."

"Are you quite done with this tedium?"

"Nowhere near done. Did your snitches happen to mention that Kirsi paid me a visit?"

Little sparks glistened in his eyes. Holy shit, Kirsi was good. She had managed to evade surveillance, or maybe she had a certain influence in her homeland.

"If they had, they would have also told you she was with Celia Trice."

Recognition flickered in his eyes. He knew who Celia was.

"You might have heard of Celia," I went on. "She's one of the most powerful diviners in all the magic world."

"Is this ever coming to a point?"

Temper, temper.

"Yes, a sharp point... Celia told me I'm related to Chaos. You wouldn't know anything about that, would you?"

He set the book he'd been holding on the coffee table. "I think I'll honor your request now and leave."

As he stood up, I blocked his way. "How is Chaos related to me? Don't act like you don't know. You practically forced him to give me his blood."

Nothing. No flickering of the eyes, not the slightest twitch of a muscle. He just stood there, expressionless.

"So that's how it's going to be," I concluded.

His eyes dipped to mine. "Of all the things to concern you, this revelation should be at the bottom of your list, Luna."

I sat on the couch. "Celia Trice wouldn't have flown all the way to Sweden to tell me if it wasn't important. I am tired of these games, Winter."

He sat next to me. "Had you asked Celia to look into your past?"

"Answering a question with a question... you had to be the guy who invented that a few millennia ago. You do it a lot. Forget it, I'll go straight to Chaos. He will not hesitate to tell me. He is *family*, after all."

He flared his nostrils, then glanced out the window. "Chaos isn't here. He left the West Coast," he said with eyes still looking away. "In fact, I believe he's left North America."

How fucking convenient.

"Not a problem. He's not the only one willing to help."

His head spun, eyes locking on mine. "What? Who?"

Aha, now he's taking this seriously.

"Oh, I thought you liked kept secrets? Last chance, big boy. Who gave me to you? How am I connected to Chaos?"

Irritation shot across his face. "You're not. You are who you choose to be, in every sense of the word, not the product of a genetic imprint."

It's like talking to a mule.

"You know, Kirsi thinks you have a soft spot for me. I said you didn't, and you've just proven me right. Because this is not how you care about someone, treating me like a child and leaving me in the dark about my true heritage which you know I struggle with."

I walked to the door, opened it wide. Winter flicked his wrist. The door banged shut.

His eyes darkened. "You couldn't have chosen a worse time to come back. Someone or something has been targeting magic and supernatural residents in San Diego county."

The sincerity on his face changed everything.

"Targeting them how?" I said.

"The victims are stripped of their abilities, then slip into a deep coma. They become completely unresponsive to both science and magic."

The world spun around me. My ears began to buzz. That hit close to home. My mother had slipped into a vegetative state after fighting off some unknown entity who was after me. A cold fear cut through me that I was to blame now as I was then. "San Diego? Why... San Diego?" I muttered.

"I can't be certain," he said. "San Diego county has an elevated density of supernatural beings, due to the weather and its proximity to an abundance of nearby portals to the Deep Down and other enchanted places, like Serenity Valley."

"That's the biggest bullshit reason ever," I said, clapping back. "You really have no respect for my intelligence, do you?"

Winter shook his head. "If you let me finish, I was going to say, there are so many to question and until we talk to everyone and find out what is out there, lurking over this city, you should return to Europe immediately. I'll summon you the moment it's safe to return."

I grimaced. "Summon me? That's old-world chauvinism for you."

A wave of impatience rolled over his features. "Your magic is too potent. It gets stronger by the minute. If a malevolent force got a whiff of your etheric essence, there's no limit to the dark powers they would unleash to drain you."

"That sounds unpleasant," I said. "Listen, I get it. It's a bad, bad world out there. It's not my first rodeo, remember? And, besides, my magic can barely be traced back to me. I know, I've tested it."

"Would you bet your life on it?"

"No, but I'd bet your life on it," I said, whiffing at a joke.

"You're not funny," he said. "And it's not just your life, it's anyone who might be standing next to you."

I hated when he was right. Winter hadn't a clue who or what was behind the strange outbreak of catatonic supernatural folk, but that was precisely why it was so unnerving. It could be anyone or anything. It could be Horror himself.

"Okay, you win, I'll think about it," I said. "I've been traveling for twenty-four hours and I need to crash before I decide anything."

I realized he was hooking his eyes onto me like a vulture.

"What?" I said.

"I'm telling you to sit this mess out. I got it covered."

How I wish that were true.

"Shit," I said. "You're worried Horror or another Eternal is involved."

"I'm not saying that."

"You didn't have to. It's written all over your face."

"Nothing is known, Luna," he said. "And nothing is needed from you on this one. And, for sure, there is nothing written on my face."

"Okay, Mr. Poker Face, I'm about done here," I said. "I'm going to sleep now for quite a few hours. If the world's still here when I wake, a decision will be forthcoming."

Winter took a breath and then walked out without saying a word.

I did not care that my reaction was inappropriate considering what he had revealed. I was delirious and not ready to be commanded. The situation he had described sounded dire. Why was I pissed at him anyway? I was so tired nothing made sense anymore.

I trudged unsteadily to call him back, swinging the door open and stepping outside. I grabbed the railing, bent over it and stretched my neck out to scan the area below. There was no sign of him.

Winter was gone. I could not even be sure he had ever been there. The whole thing had started to feel like a nightmare.

Chapter 2

THE COFFEE SHOP WAS packed with customers chattering over John Mayer's breathy vocals, texting as they waited for their drinks, while others worked on laptops with stoic faces, diligently shutting out all the hubbub.

Big Rob noticed me at the door. He raised a hand behind the counter to get my attention, mouthing out *later* before taking the next order.

It seemed like years had passed since I worked behind that counter, often by Rob's side, but it had only been six soul-crushing, life-changing months.

Someone lay a hand on my shoulder and turned me around. I yelped with excitement to see Faion there smiling radiantly.

I wrapped my arms around him and hugged him tight.

"Good to see you, too, moon baby," he said as he took a step back to give me the once over.

"What?" I said.

"Those Scandinavians have you eating right?" he said, furrowing his brow. "Are you getting your iron? Sleeping enough?"

His voice melted my heart. "Um, yes, *Dad*... if I didn't know better, it sounds like you actually missed me."

"Okay, yeah, sure," he said, unconvincingly, "but what I'm saying is you don't look so hot, it's like you're a Walking Dead character we forgot about until they returned late in the season as a walker, all skinny and pale with dark sunken eyes."

I punched his shoulder. "Dude, I had a transcontinental flight."

He nodded. "Yeah, I know, I'm with that. I'm just saying... were you on *Zombie Airlines*? Because, I mean, you ragged, girl."

I laughed. "So, I'm a bit tattered. I haven't had my coffee yet."

"I'm messing with you," he said. "You still look like a favorite teller at a frat boys' spank bank."

It was good luck that instant cell regeneration didn't kick in unless my body experienced substantial physical trauma. I was grateful that I could still look tired and mortal. I missed that feeling of fitting in.

"You're ridiculous," I said.

Faion grinned. "Thank you."

He took my hand and led me to a table. A lean young man with untidy brown hair, wearing a gray SDSU AZTECS t-shirt and wrinkled khakis, stood up and flashed me a hearty smile. He was handsome in a boyish way, the kind of guy who'd offer his arm to an old lady to help her cross a street.

"Sophie, meet Joey," Faion said.

Joey extended his hand. "Charmed," he said. "Faion says fantastic things about you. He thinks you're fearless and gorgeous."

Faion slapped Joey's wrist. "I said she loco as fuck, chases trouble like it's chocolate and I have to be rescuing her little ass all the time."

"Blah blah, we both know what you meant," Joey said.

"I'm dating a guy who says *blah blah*," Faion said, shaking his head.

"It's true, Joey," I assured him. "Faion's speaking the truth. I'm about as crazy as a girl can be. First I act, then, maybe, I might think a little."

"So, you're both crazy?" Joey said, almost disappointed.

"I'm afraid so."

Faion arched an eyebrow. "Did both of you just call me crazy?"

Joey chuckled. "I'm going to let you two catch up," he said. "It was a complete pleasure meeting you, Sophie."

"Same here."

Joey squeezed Faion's hand. "See you in a bit," he said.

Faion leaned in for a quick kiss. Their ease and comfort with each other sent a pang of longing through my core.

I need that in my life.

I crossed my arms as Joey walked away. "Okay, how come I'm just finding out now about a boyfriend you've obviously had for a while?"

Faion shrugged. "The last few months have been a dream, girlfriend. I forgot about the rest of the world, if I'm being honest. *Who are you, again?*" He laughed. "Love can reduce the planet down to two beating hearts."

Asshole. That was so damn lovely. *I want that.* "Sounds serious."

Faion took a sip of his Frappuccino. "We're in a good place."

Holding his tongue was not typical Faion. I would have expected him to be chomping at the bit to deluge me with a frenzied retelling of events.

It must be serious.

I squinted, then gave him my sweetest smile. "A place called love?"

He thought about it. "That's not me. I'm not going to put a name on it, wrap it up and freeze it in the icebox. Nah. It's just good. I don't need to conquer and label it. You got to let things breathe if you want them to live."

Wow.

"That's wisdom," I said. "He's *basic*, right?"

"He is what he is, but yeah."

Dating a basic had a whole lunch box full of complications for us Deep Downers. Lines could get blurred very fast.

I was the last person to give relationship advice, but I did anyway. "That could work, just be careful. I worry about you."

"Just be careful?" Faion repeated. "Said the girl who runs around with wolves and old-ass Neanderthal dudes. How about you, huh? Did you catch any dick in Stockholm?"

"Jeez," I said. "No, I did not catch anything of the like. I'm not even thinking about guys."

"Okay, now you're lying," he said with a raised eyebrow. "You still thinking about Mr. Freeze Pop."

Not in that way. Farthest thing from my mind. Really.

My priorities lined up far away from romance. I was much more concerned with things like who my real parents were, why they abandoned me, and what my connection was to a deranged Immortal apocalypse junkie whose agenda could very well include eliminating me after I was of no use to him. You know, the basic stuff that concerns all recent grads.

"What's this?" I said. "Now that you have a boyfriend you have to mess with single people? Happy people are total snobs."

He laughed. "Okay, you right."

"Yeah, I *am* right," I said, thrilled to be talking to my friend again.

Big Rob walked up to our table offering me a cranberry orange scone.

I snatched it out of his hands. "Oh, man, I missed these," I said, munching on the delicious warmth of the scone.

"My god, Sophie," Rob said. "Slow down, you'll choke."

"Dude," I said with my mouth full. "You remembered my scone."

Faion eyed Big Rob. "That's because you the bullet in Rambo's gun."

Rob did not find Faion amusing. "Is this guy bothering you, Soph?"

I nodded. "Totally. Throw him out. He's making fun of me because I'm single."

Rob seemed completely confused. "You're single?"

Faion rolled his eyes. "Oh, here we go," he said under his breath.

Rob ignored him. "They treating you well over in Europe? If not, tell them they'll have to come answer to me."

Faion scrunched his face and held his heart mockingly.

"Thanks, Rob," I said. "Yeah. They're nice. I'm good."

"Well, okay then," Rob said, trying to form a sexy smile. "And I know you were joking about your friend here bothering you."

Faion smiled at Rob who nodded to Faion.

"Oh no, I totally wasn't," I said.

Rob stood uneasy on his feet, uncertain. "Right," he said with a nervous laugh and then slowly walked back to the customers.

I took a deep breath in. "I miss my life," I said. "I miss San Diego."

"You're being compulsive," Faion said. "It will wear off."

"I'm not being compulsive."

"You just ate that San Diego scone in fifteen seconds. That's compulsive. You're bingeing on nostalgia."

"Okay, so what? I never asked for any of this shit, and you know it."

Faion pulled me to his chest for a hug. "Yeah, I know."

"That's better," I said.

He let me keep my head on his chest for a while and I wanted to stay in his embrace forever.

"Saw your girlfriend Tam the other day," he said.

I lifted my head and stared at him. "*My* Tam?"

"Yeah."

"Oh, cool. How's she doing?"

My childhood best friend, Tam Nguyen, was one of the most uniquely skilled lunar witches and an absolute breath of fresh air among the deep dwellers. She could also outrun a rabbit and shoot the eyes off a peacock's tail with an arrow.

"Promoted up the Lunar ranks. Sounds like she's mad busy," Faion said.

Primary level witch at twenty-three? Who did that?

Tam did, obviously. Every year she broke a record. Primary level meant she had developed complete control over nocturnal elements and could now manipulate that energy in multiple ways.

"Total legend," I said. "Wish I could see her, but I only have eight days."

Faion stared at me. "Hey, I might come visit you. Joey's doing a semester abroad at Sotheby's Institute of Art in

London. I might tag along. We'd practically be neighbors."

I arched an eyebrow. "Tag along? With Joey?"

"What?"

"That sounds serious, buddy."

"Nah," he said. "It's not about that. I'm looking for context. I need to expand my horizons, drink up some culture. Educate myself, you dig? If I have a greater understanding of societal strata and what not, I can decide what I want to do with my life. I'm thinking film studies or architecture."

So proud right now.

"Faion, I love it. Good for you. That's awesome, really. In fact, I wish you could leave tomorrow."

He tilted his head. "Are you trying to get rid of me?"

Shit. I'm not smooth.

"Faion..." I tried to find the right words. "Go with Joey. Go early. San Diego isn't safe right now. There have been several attacks on supernaturals and magics alike. Have you heard about it? They think it's all orchestrated."

His face told me he was clueless. "No, I haven't. But what about you? Who told you this? You've been gone."

"Obviously, Winter told me."

Faion shook his head. "That dude's bad news."

"He told me to go back to Europe."

"Yeah, I'm sure he did, because he knew you wouldn't go," Faion said. "You don't think that a guy that old knows how to cleverly manipulate?"

"I know who and what Winter is, Faion, but I make my

own choices."

"That's what everybody thinks. What did the generous purveyor of information tell you?"

"There have been incidents all over San Diego county," I said, taking a deep breath. "The victims lose their magic, then they slip into a coma."

"Okay, and why San Diego in particular?"

"Winter speculates," I said, wishing I hadn't brought up his name, "that the density of supernatural elements in the area could be a factor."

"That's a total guess, but whatever, it's not good."

"Not at all. Please, be safe, Faion, until we know what we're dealing with. Don't be out at night alone and stay near public places. Talk to Celia soon, okay? She might know something."

"What about your grandmother?"

I shrugged. "She was supposed to fly down for Easter, but now I'm not sure that's the best idea."

Faion crossed his arms and shook his head. "I can't believe you've survived this long. You're like a harbinger. Every time I see you, I know shit is about to get real, too real, scary real. You're a disaster magnet."

One hundred percent.

My phone buzzed. It was Celia texting me. I read the text quietly, a pang of guilt rushing to my face for not telling Faion it was from his grandmother.

"I guess, according to you, I better go get some beauty

sleep, so I don't drag around looking like a zombie. Let's talk tomorrow?"

"Cool," Faion said. "And that whole thing about you being fearless, that's not always a good thing."

"I'll stay out of trouble," I said, eager to get going. "Promise."

"I am choosing to believe that," he said. "And, me too."

Celia had just confirmed my appointment with the powerful seer for me. She was going to accompany me to the designated location at eight o'clock the next morning. I tried to wipe the guilt off my face.

A quick hug and Faion was gone. Joey waved back to me as the happy couple left the coffee shop. I wished my life could be that simple, a warm hand to hold, a trip to the coffee shop with the one you love, a lazy afternoon together as one.

I floated toward the door in a daze when I bumped into a skinny guy carrying a bunch of textbooks under one arm. His coffee cup flew out of his other hand. A spark of magic left my fingers to envelop the cup in midflight and deliver it directly to my right hand.

"I'm sorry," I said, handing the coffee back to the stunned guy.

Magic was a bad idea.

I scampered out the door on edge. Somehow, I already knew who would be waiting on my doorstep when I got back home.

Chapter 3

WINTER SPRANG TO HIS feet as soon as he saw me, his six-foot-two frame looming over me. He was rather disheveled with his loose gray sweats, fitted black tank top, sweat-glistened biceps and messy blond hair. Apparently, he had been hitting the gym often and I doubted it had anything to do with physical conditioning. No, Winter was trying to work through stress and tension.

I shoved him aside to get to the door. He uniquely triggered my most primitive, immature responses.

"Is this how it's going to be now?" I said without looking at him. "You're just going to pop by uninvited?"

His warm breath on the back of my neck sent a shiver through me.

"When I call, you don't answer," he said. "So, I stopped calling."

"I'm not a prisoner to my phone like everybody else."

I unlocked the door, stepped inside and started to close it behind me.

I laughed when he wedged his foot between the door and the frame. I let go of the door and let him follow me inside.

"This is urgent," he said, darting his eyes about the place.

"Isn't it always? That's like the stalker's creed. The concept of boundaries means nothing."

He placed his hands on my shoulders and spun me around until we came face to face. "The attacks have escalated. There have been five assaults in the past twenty-four hours. Five, Luna!"

The concern on my face must have been obvious because he released my shoulders and softened his approach. "There's something else."

I felt my heartbeat surging. "What else?"

"A death," he said. "The first."

"What? Who, Jonas?"

"A wind mage slipped away after three days in a delirious state."

I buried my face in my hands. "Oh, the poor soul. Listen, you're not chasing me back to Europe. I'm staying."

He fought the urge to respond but, instead, exhaled forcefully. "This is going to spread from the basic world. I believe all this is a test of power and the real target will be the Deep Down."

"If you had told me sooner, I might have been able to do something. Your spies in Stockholm could have told me any day," I said.

"Let's keep it in the present."

"Fine, the present," I said, losing my patience. "Tell me exactly what happens during and after one of these attacks."

He walked to the window. "The victims are isolated. They probably feel a tingling sensation like their limbs are falling asleep and then they are paralyzed in place. If they're standing, they do not fall right away. It's painful and feels like the pain lasts for an hour, but it's over in a matter of seconds."

"With unresponsive victims," I said, trying to understand, "how do you know such details? Was there a witness?"

"Not that I know of," he said.

"Okay, then a seer must have been brought in?"

"No. I mean, yeah, I've been told that in some cases seers were brought in, but they saw nothing. There's a total lockdown of the victim's consciousness."

"Then what? This is a theory you pulled from where? Your ass?"

He turned and shook his head. "Is that how a lady should talk?"

"In this world? Yes."

He sighed and stared into my eyes. "There are a few cryptic references in surviving archives mentioning similar events almost 5500 years ago during the Neolithic decline."

My jaw dropped. "And you just jumped from there to this thing six millennia later without hesitation? Have you ever heard of scholarly method? Because your proof is so damn anecdotal and useless. And, besides, the Neolithic decline was about a huge drop in human population, not a few catatonic magical beings."

"It's just a theory," he said.

"No, it's really not," I said. "Alright, forget that, what happens to these victims after the attacks?"

"They lose their ability to access magical energy from anywhere and become comatose. Out of twenty-four known cases, twenty-three have remained in the exact state in which they were found. The wind mage took a turn and was gone within ten minutes. The only clue we have is the fine silver dust that hangs in the air at the scenes of the attacks. The dust is toxic to anyone who uses magic. In light of this, the Seventh Council has decided not to get directly involved. Officially, we're monitoring the situation from a distance."

"Ah, convenient isolationists," I said, not one bit surprised.

"Immortals are not the most altruistic beings."

"That's an understatement," I said. "You guys are like supercharged survivalist nut bags."

"I'll assume that's not a compliment," he said. "And I agree, it's a mistake. This silver dust is potent enough to affect Immortals, to a lesser extent. I felt its power while at a scene. It was a nagging force, scratching at my etheric essence. I did manage with some effort to block it."

"I know where this is headed. I told you I'm not leaving."

He hesitated. "Okay."

Huh?

"Did you just say, *okay?*"

He nodded. "I wish there was another way. I need your help, Luna. We need to act fast. This will spread if we don't neutralize the attacking force before they grow too strong. We don't know much about silver dust, but I doubt it has anticipated the rare morning magic of the mist riders. Your growing command of mist craft and earth energy could be our secret weapon."

I picked up a couch cushion and held it to my chest. The Deep Down Board of Supernatural Orders had been fearful of this kind of scenario ever since I could remember—an invisible plague, an airborne menace that would attack our essence and our power centers, which are intimately connected to our consciousness. Our subterranean world hadn't faced such a malignant threat in centuries.

I gave Winter a weary stare. "And you told the magistrates what you've told me?"

"Of course. It didn't matter. They're keeping a watchful eye. That's it."

"How has the Deep Down responded to the crisis?"

Winter shrugged. "Don't know. I'm persona non grata in your magic realm, I'm afraid. I might have reached out to Iris, but you're here."

"Yeah, I'll talk to her." I held the cushion and yelled into it before tossing it back onto the couch. "I'm so sick of evil idiots."

Faion was obviously clueless of the attacks when we spoke. The silver dust threat must have been kept classified in order to avoid panic.

"In every era, the final dance partners are always good and evil," Winter said.

I rubbed my temples. "Do we have any of this dust?"

"One small vial in my lab, completely shielded. It's toxic to all magic users, Luna. It sucks up etheric energy like a fusion reactor. Get too close to it, and the effect is almost certainly irreversible. Basics seem to be unaffected as their essence is so primitive and impotent."

A supernatural dust that robbed witches, mages, diviners and all other wielders of magic of their very essence before it killed them. What malevolent bastard could even think something like that up?

One name comes to mind.

"Düsternis," I said. "Don't know why, but his name just popped into my head. That would explain why the Seventh Council is staying out of it... because they're behind the whole damn thing."

Winter pushed back his sweaty hair. "No. It's not him."

"You just rule him out without a doubt? I see. Blind faith. He's the leader of your cult and all that. He's given up on you, but you haven't given up on him. Is that how it is? Really? You know what, true believer? He probably has his best boy Argos out dispersing Shaervas with canisters of the evil dust to drop off at every Deep Down portal as we speak."

The thought of Shaervas made my skin crawl. The ancient ice snakes were instruments for clandestine witchcraft that could adulterate magic sources, infusing them with dark energy. Argos had tried to use them before to infiltrate the Deep Down, on Düsternis' orders, but Chaos had put an end to that plan.

Winter paced the room. "That's cute, but I'm not drinking the Immortal Kool-Aid. I told you, the dust is not impartial to my kind. The only reason I can shield my etheric essence is the resistance and discipline training only the Umbra Order practices. Most Immortals don't have that ability."

Shadow Warriors were the most skillful controllers of elemental magic and ley line energy among Immortals. They were also quicker to violence and could kill other Immortals by dragging out their essence. From the handful of apprentices who tried, only a few ever managed to get through all Umbra rites of passage and become initiates. Among that small number were Winter and Chaos. They had a very useful and timely skillset for such times.

I stared at him. "And once again you've gone rogue from your own council. Why?"

Winter stepped closer. "I think you know that answer."

I knew *part* of the answer. He had proven more than once to be on my side and an ally to the Lunar Order.

"But us working together is not ideal, you must admit," I said. "Why not bring in Kirsi or even Chazona, for all I care?"

Ugh. I hate when my subconscious betrays me.

Why on Earth did I bring that wicked bitch up? Her utter delight at taunting me with her possible intimacy with Winter still burned deep red holes in my brain.

Winter's eye twitched. "Perhaps it's time you extinguish all petty rivalries that serve no purpose, Luna. Just because our dalliance didn't pan out as you had hoped, doesn't mean we can't come together in a time of crisis."

Dude, what? I can't believe he went there.

I stared at him, dumfounded. "First, I can't unpack all the delusions you loaded into what you just said. That better have been a failed joke. I mean, get over yourself. I could write a book about the reasons I don't want to partner up with you for anything. *Anything*, Winter. Sheesh. Every time I try to put the broken pieces of my life back together, you're always right here in my face wanting to rip it all apart again. You lie, manipulate, annoy, stalk, mislead, withhold key information and drip with arrogance. And you're sweaty. Why do you come over here and sweat all over everything? This is not the resume of my ideal partner, okay? I think we can agree on that at least."

He peered into my eyes, wearily. "I misspoke. Forgive me."

Talking to him was like racing through a minefield. I walked to the door. "Yeah, it's time for you to go. You wear me out. *Man.* I'll sleep on it, okay? Best I can offer right now.'

He walked past me without a glance. "It's not about me,

in the end. Luna Mae is a mist rider and mist riders never turn away."

Winter closed the door quietly behind him. He was wrong. It wasn't the mist rider who wanted to turn away, it was the girl. It was self-preservation.

I needed a drink, a stiff drink or three. And then I needed to talk to Celia's friend, Penelope Osvaldo, seer extraordinaire.

Chapter 4

THE LITTLE HOUSE IN El Cajon sat atop a hill. Moss, clover and grass crept from the cracks of the steep steps that led up to a faded aquamarine door. Untidy boxwood hedges shot upwards on both sides. With my elbow cradled around Celia's, I guided her up one uneven step at a time.

A brass lionhead door knocker greeted us at eye level and a little porch to our left was busy with multicolored pots of parsley, basil, fennel and more.

Celia knocked on the door. Sounds of cats meowing and feet shuffling led to the door opening slowly with a creak. The petite, older woman who faced us seemed strangely familiar.

Her timeworn face studied mine with a sense of recognition.

"Dear friend," she said, turning to Celia, "what notable *bruja* have you brought to me? It must be Luna Mae of Astoria, once a witch and now *mucho más,*" she said with a clear, melodic accent.

Celia nodded. "Yes, Penelope, Luna Mae is my grandson's school friend and a very darling girl."

The fact Celia talked so formally while using such casual affectations struck a false chord. It felt rehearsed.

Penelope Osvaldo sunk her inquisitive eyes into mine. "If you wish to pass through the doors of perception, darling witch, you must leave your earthly needs outside. *Deja tu cuerpo.*"

Leave my body? Um, okay... whatever.

I followed Celia inside. When the door closed, we stood in a dark hallway.

"Come," Penelope said. "Let's talk."

Instinctively, I followed the sound of the seer's footsteps to a small sitting room crammed with Rococo furniture. It felt like we were stepping into an 18th century French boudoir—complete with a sofa, two gilded wood-framed chairs upholstered in leaf-patterns, worn leather-bound tomes displayed behind glass, and mahogany console tables decorated with porcelain figurines.

Two enormous white Persian cats rubbed their backs against Penelope's calves. Despite her advanced age, the seer was lithe and glided over the plush carpet with the grace of a retired tap dancer. She was not wearing a tuxedo or galoshes this time, but it would be hard to forget her small, intense eyes and the tangled web of fine wrinkles across her forehead. Penelope Osvaldo was none other than Lucia's eccentric friend that I had met at the same New Year's Eve party where Winter had tried to determine whether Chaos had hijacked Lucia's mind again or not.

A strong wave of energy washed over me, my stomach lunged, and my breath caught in my chest. Someone or something was testing my strength. I held back my magic, not wanting to give away too much, allowing the wave of energy to run through my entire body unchallenged.

Penelope opened the lid of a teapot sitting atop a tall, golden samovar. Steam rose to her face as she bent over to inhale the escaping aromas.

"May I offer you some tea?" she said, eyes closed, enjoying the rich scent of the fresh brew.

Celia beamed. "Yes, indeed. How charming!" she said, directing me to the sofa to sit.

The strange concoction inside the bone china teacup re-sembled anything but tea. It was a dark grape color and syrupy with a pungent smell like boiled cabbage mixed with walnuts and, maybe, squid ink.

Penelope poured more steaming water into my cup. It did nothing to mitigate the assault on my olfactory system. I would have never put that into my mouth if not for Celia's eyes urging me to act polite.

When the hot liquid hit my tongue, my head jerked back-wards. A distant memory triggered within me like a stagger-ing déjà vu, dredging up emotions from early childhood.

I knew that taste, that persistent nutty sweetness lingering in the back of my throat. My mother (*or was it Gram?*) baked sugary green tea and walnut cupcakes that I could never stop eating. Penelope's muddy tea tasted exactly like those cupcakes!

"Each of my guests taste different things when they ingest my brew," Penelope said as if reading my mind. "What is it that you taste, Luna?"

Getting right to the spells, I see.

"Sugary green tea and walnut cupcakes," I said.

Penelope squinted. "Walnuts. Not among my favored snacks. Too much phytic acid which impairs mineral absorption. A woman my age needs her iron and zinc."

"But this isn't actually walnut," I said.

She smiled, stiffly, unimpressed with my response.

"An excellent cup of tea as always, Penelope," Celia said, trying to change the mood. "You haven't lost your special touch."

Penelope sighed. "This one never tells me what she tastes. Perhaps I should stop serving her." She lifted her open palms to her ears. "The tick tock deafens. Can you not hear it, Celia?"

Celia nodded.

What?

"I don't hear a thing," I said.

Penelope furrowed her brow. "Tick tock goes the seconds by. Tick tock the bomb blows high."

Oh, I get it. She's crazy.

"There's a bomb?"

"Yes," she said. "And the wires all run through you, my dear."

"Don't scare the child," Celia said, sternly.

Penelope reached out to pat my hand. "Never avoid the ingraining lessons of fear, youngling, only fools do that."

I stared at her hand on mine. "You're saying I'm a ticking bomb?"

Penelope waved away my words with a flick of her wrist. "Predestination is a strong magic, but there's always a way around, a forbidden passage paid with regret."

Her reassurances were not so reassuring.

"Okay, good tip," I said. "Now, how and why did you become acquainted with my best friend's mother? Don't tell me *coincidence*."

Penelope leaned back in her chair. "There are no coincidences in this world except the ones you make room for." She looked to Celia, amused.

My patience ran thin. "I'd like an answer, please."

The seer narrowed her eyes. "My interest in you is not recent. It was renewed after a conversation with Celia last fall, but I never forgot the child whom Clara Mae protected against a staggering evil."

I set my teacup on the table, worried that the anger rushing to my fingertips might explode it into a thousand pieces.

"What do you know of my mother?"

"She more than knew of her, Luna. She was there," Celia

said. "She was brought in to consult on Clara Mae's case. If anyone could have broken the necromantic spell, it would have been Penelope."

How do I unpack all this new information?

"Necromantic spell? What? Why have I never heard about this? And why involve Lucia? Why not come straight to me?"

The table shook. My cup clicked against the saucer furiously.

Celia shot me a stern look. "Easy, child. This house will not tolerate unbridled magic."

This house? I knew enchanted houses existed. I just never expected to ever be in one, especially one so peacefully placed in the basic world.

"I'm not a child, Celia. If you only knew what I've been through."

Penelope motioned to Celia to yield the floor. "I saw no point in unsettling you with sad stories of your mother. I needed only a moment in your presence, and I found that on New Year's Eve." She stopped and crossed her arms on her chest.

"And you couldn't have just bumped into me at the market?"

"I sensed extraordinary power emanating from you," she continued, ignoring my comment. "Far greater even than the grim Shadow who was your date. Far, far greater."

"That wasn't a date," I said under my breath.

"I've been trying to decide what you are ever since," Penelope said.

Alarm stabbed through my stomach. The conversation had taken a wrong turn. If I had any sense, I would have left that enchanted house and never looked back. But I needed to know if I was related to Chaos and that need overrode every warning my instincts screamed at me.

"You were asked to help with my mother's case?"

The seer gave me a half smile. "I was to penetrate Clara's consciousness to discover who was responsible for the necromantic spell. I failed, but I might have better luck with you."

I resisted the urge to hope. "You had no luck with my mother. What makes you think it'll be any different with me?"

"Because no necromantic spell was cast on you. Of this, I'm certain."

I shook my head. "I was four years old. My memory was shielded by my mother. There's nothing there."

The old seer grimaced. "Even *nothing* tells a story."

Goosebumps prickled down my arms. "I'm not here for that."

"I know, dear, Celia has filled me in."

As if on cue, Celia rose to her feet. "I'll remove myself to the kitchen."

Penelope took a sip of tea. "Shall we begin? You desire details from your past that have been kept from you, yes?"

A premonition overtook me. "You warned there'd be a price to pay. Celia mentioned that, too."

"Negotiating with the preternatural is not all wine and roses."

I couldn't argue with that. "So, what cost?"

"Ah, it's never so easy," she said. "Ask yourself this: What is precious and what would you be willing to part with?"

The people in my life are all that matters.

I pursed my lips. "I'm not going to murder anyone for you. Or steal government secrets, or anything crazy like that," I added for good measure.

"No, that won't be necessary. What I want must come from you and it must be given freely."

That did not sound good. "Can you be more precise?"

She leaned back, locking her eyes on mine. "That which is yet to come, that which you will cherish, that which will complete you."

No more riddles... please!

"Fresh tamales? My master's degree? A cute new blouse?"

A dark green aura flared around the seer. "A child, Luna Mae, that is the price I will exert. Not your first child and not your last child. Not a female child. A son. Not your second and not your fourth. Your third son."

Okay, now we were entering cloud cuckoo land. My initial impression of her at Lucia's party when she used a pink umbrella as a walking stick still seemed spot on. She lived in her own reality. Completely.

"Bringing children into this messed-up world isn't a priority right now," I said, holding her penetrating stare.

And even if I did have children, I wouldn't be so stupid as to keep having them after I had two boys. Easy fix. She was probably in her seventies and mortal. What were the chances that I'd have not one, not two, but three sons while she still drew breath? I could wait her out and she knew that. What was the catch?

"It is the price," she insisted. "Your third son."

As far as deranged demands went, it wasn't highly original. I'd read tons of stories and seen tons of movies where a child was used as a bargaining chip. "When you say you want him, what do you mean, exactly?"

"I will come to collect the boy when he turns seven."

Like I said, cuckoo land. "And what if I don't honor my promise?"

"The child will perish before he reaches adulthood."

Nice, except I was immortal and if I ever had a child, it wouldn't be with a mortal. If I could avoid the grief of watching a lover or a husband die, I would. My children would be immortal, or I wouldn't have them, period.

"Why do you want a son of mine?"

"That I will not reveal." Her eyes turned stone cold. "What will it be, Luna Mae?"

There was no point worrying over a hypothetical child that might or might not exist. Penelope Osvaldo had no idea what I was, what I was capable of, but I did. She didn't stand a chance against me.

"Let it be so," I said. "If ever I have three sons, the third one will be yours as long as you swear in blood the child will be safe and well cared for."

A pleased smile crossed the seer's face. One of the Persian cats jumped into her lap with a growl. Penelope caressed the cat. "I release my Order oath that I will do anything in my power to protect the child from the dark evils of the world known and the worlds unknown."

She grabbed the cat by the scruff of the neck and lifted it to shoulder's height. Purple flames enveloped the animal and the seer's hand. The cat screeched and twisted before vanishing out of sight.

A pool of blood stretched out in ripples underneath Penelope's feet, staining the carpet.

Not a cat after all, a shapeshifting Northern pixie. She would bind the oath and return to life in her original form at the next full moon.

The light went out in the room. Penelope lit a beeswax candle held by an old brass holder. She pricked her left index finger with a letter opener. A drop of blood fell into the flame, burning up with a hissing sound.

Penelope offered me the letter opener. "Now your oath."

Everything I was ever taught, all the instruction and training I had received, everything that I was, and everything the Lunar Order stood for, screamed at me that magic oaths were binding and not to be taken lightly.

There's a first time for everything.

The candle flame lapped up the drop of my blood like an eager tongue, flaming higher as if hungry for more. I focused in on the shield I had around my etheric essence, hoping it would withstand the seer's penetrating powers.

"There's a very powerful Immortal related to me," I said. "They call him Chaos. His blood runs in my veins. Literally. I want to know for sure if we really are related by more than a blood transfusion."

A shadow darkened the seer's face. "His blood will guide me." Her gaze latched onto me like a hook. "I give you a second and final chance to change the course of destiny. You can still bow out, no strings attached."

I shook my head. "The future of our world is at stake. Continue."

Penelope sat back in her chair and closed her eyes which fluttered under her eyelids. Her lips quivered. I saw the aura around her flicker and fade. Then the aura puffed up like a marshmallow and charged at me.

I clutched onto the sofa cushion to keep me from running away. When the prickly aura pushed its way through the pores of my skin, it felt like tiny needles stabbing me all over my body.

Penelope drew a sudden breath. "I stare into depths of darkness, feel unfathomable despair, hear an indecipherable language of evil muting a whimpering anguish. A child's heartbeat cutting through it all."

I held my breath, scared to interrupt her.

"I sense the Immortal moving inside your blood," she said. Her tone had become emotionless, like a virtual assistant. "His markers mingle in your cell structures all the way to your magic core. You are of the same kind, the connection with him is profound and binding. First or second degree relative likely, third degree at the most."

What were first degree relatives? Parents, children, siblings? Then you had cousins, uncles, grandparents, grandchildren, half-siblings. The revelation overwhelmed me, overloading me with stress. I chuckled involuntarily.

"Your amusement seems inappropriate."

Penelope's reprimand brought me to my senses. It wasn't funny, but in a weird way—the weirdest of ways—it made sense. From the very beginning, Chaos had treated me with kid gloves, calling me affectionate nicknames, never lifting a finger to defend himself when I attacked, figuring out the Sacred Vault situation for me, using the third-eye vision at great risk to himself in order to locate Emmet, and then rushing to the Sacred Vault to get me out of there alive and even assuming the whole blame.

It suddenly dawned on me—the *son of a bitch* cared.

What was he to me? What was I to him? How did I get this so wrong?

"There is more," Penelope said. "It was Chaos himself, the Lord of the Demon Hounds, the most villainous of the Shadows, who handed you over to the Seventh Council

Chief Magistrate Winter twenty-two years ago."

My hands grew cold. I struggled to breathe. I felt an abyss opening in my core that threatened to swallow me whole.

Chaos was Lord of the black demon hounds? Did I hear that right?

Lords were born half-divine and their powers were immeasurable according to the most ancient scrolls held in the Central Museum of the Lower Realms. The hellhounds, as they were commonly known, had been rumored to be sniffing around the very portals of the exile vortex itself, but that was just a subterranean legend most viewed as nothing more than folklore.

The first Lord of the black demon hounds was Darius, known in the up above as the Third Persian King of Kings. Darius had stepped down weeks before vanishing completely almost one thousand years ago.

How do you destroy the undestroyable? That oft quoted line on the playgrounds at magic school was referring to Darius (in the *Fifth Almanac of the Melded Ages*, I believe). Darius had obviously chosen to go, but magic kind had never completely accepted it.

Penelope had to be wrong. There was no way Chaos was his successor. That would make him a demigod, and if that was true, why would he have ever become Horror's sidekick?

And why would I be in his possession as a baby? And why would he give me to Winter whom he antagonized? None of that made one bit of sense.

Penelope's body contorted violently. Her eyes snapped open. Her irises had narrowed down to black slits. "I can't go any deeper," she said. "The telepathic channel is collapsed here. Most unfortunate. Some more tea?"

I watched as she got up and walked to the samovar, cheerfully. Nothing felt real—not the enchanted house, not the seer's nonsensical words or, for sure, not her awkward hospitality.

Suddenly, I was sinking. Everything I thought I knew started to fall to pieces and, once again, I found myself needing Winter. Only he could provide any clarity at all. I finally had an inkling as to why he had been so unwilling to share more of my past. My lineage was unspeakable—all terror and darkness.

I raised my hand. "No tea. Thank you, Penelope. Am I right to assume you can't tell me the precise familial relationship I have with Chaos?"

The seer grew sympathetic. "I've told all."

"Okay, yeah. This helped, but now I must go."

Penelope gripped my wrist, gently. "A word of advice?"

"I don't know. What will it cost me?"

"No cost, *dulce niña*. A path of gloom and doom can be a path of knowledge for the strong and true. Never forget that every Shadow is a distortion. Their direction can change with the hour. Especially the Shadow you trust."

"I think I understand," I said. "Trust no one."

She heaved a deep sigh. "You are young, but your light

is strong, too strong to dance with shadows. It's a most dangerous game you two are playing. Grab only at what you can touch... or your hands will remain ever empty."

Chapter 5

I SAT WITH CELIA on the terrace of a little Italian café. A playful breeze skipped across the marble top tables and fluttered in the burnt orange umbrellas protecting us from the sun.

Celia had suggested lunch near campus under the guise of waiting for Faion to finish his last class of the day. I agreed even though my tormented mind made me anything but social.

I picked at the French toast with my fork, distracted by the traffic on the street beyond the green rail. I was processing so many things that I couldn't hold a train of thought for three seconds.

Celia studied me over her strawberry and poppyseed salad. "Call your grandmother, Sophie. You don't have to figure this all out on your own. Iris is a witch who has seen much in her days."

I'd love to pick Gram's brain about the seer's revelations,

but the more people who knew about my connection to Chaos, the harder it would be to conceal it from Düsternis's scrutiny. Gram would also love to help, no doubt, but the unrest in her energy and her attempts to investigate could unleash a chain reaction of dire consequences.

I took a sip from my tall glass of mint chocolate shake. "How well do you know Penelope?" I said. "I mean, do you completely trust her?"

Celia shrugged. "It is not Penelope Osvaldo you trust or distrust. It's her gift. A seer may use their abilities to acquire power, but they would never lie about or alter what they have seen. There's an unbreakable sanctity to their visions, a deep state of meditation that once betrayed would be lost to them forever. Whatever she told you and whatever price you paid, it's all real."

I promised my third son to a seer. How messed up is that?

"Sophie, are you feeling okay?"

I nodded. "Yeah," I said, trying to get it together. "Penelope gave me a warning. She clearly suggested Winter is the most dangerous man on Earth, at least as far as I'm concerned."

Why did I tell Celia that? Not smart, but the benevolence in her eyes made me want to pour my heart out and earn a reassuring smile. A few encouraging words from her would be milk and honey to my soul.

Celia raised an eyebrow. "And is that really a revelation, dear?"

Huh. She had a strong point.

My eyes jumped from Celia to a vision in a green beach dress.

"You better hope your plane went down or your phone was stolen," Lily said as she floated toward me, beaming her perfect smile.

She slid into the chair between Celia and me.

Happiness buzzed through my chest. "Lil, I wasn't ghosting you, I swear. I had to shake jet lag and get a few things out of the way."

"Save it, Collinsworth," Lily said. "I've heard it all before."

Her forced smile didn't hide the reproach in her voice. Lily had texted me twice since I'd been back and though I'd been dying to meet up with her, I failed even to respond. Too much silver dust in my eyes, I guess.

I tucked my hair behind my ear. "Lily, this is Celia, Faion's grandmother."

Lily's eyes widened. "Miss Celia," she said. "It's so nice to meet you. Faion talks about you a lot."

"Very kind of you, Lily," Celia said. "It's a comfort to know Faion has so many goodhearted friends."

"He's so fun," Lily said, her easy manner returning. "A whole lot more fun than little Miss Serious here."

"That's not fair to compare me to Faion," I said.

"Oh, yeah, because he returns my texts," Lily said.

"You're both adorable and obviously love each other," Celia said. "Life's too short for such trivialities."

Lily and I looked at each other, then broke out laughing.

"That's the *Miss Celia wisdom* Faion always talks about," Lily said.

I took Lily's hand and held it. "I'm sorry, Lil. Celia's right. I love you so much. Totally, completely, awkwardly."

"*Awkward*," Lily said. "At least that part's spot on."

Celia smiled. "Now I see it, you're both knuckleheads like my grandson. It's all starting to make sense."

Lily squeezed my hand. "Love reciprocated."

"Aww," I said.

"I can't stay mad at you," Lily said. "Especially when I have gossip."

"Gossip? What?"

Lily rolled her eyes. "I think Lucia has a new mystery man."

Oh no. This better not be... Zack Wisdom. I warned Chaos never to go near Lucia again. If he did, I was going to bring the moon down on his head.

"And, oh yeah," Lily continued, "you'll never guess who I bumped into. I'll give you a clue. He's the one that got away and he's a doctor!"

"Emmet?"

"Yeah, Emmet. Did you date any other hot doctors?"

Before I could respond, Celia threw her head back and began to murmur. Her eyes moved rapidly underneath her closed eyelids. Her hands trembled as she clutched onto the table edge.

"Sophie, what's happening?" Lily said. "Is she having a seizure?"

I shook my head. I was dumbstruck. "Don't know." I took Celia's hands into mine. "Miss Celia, it's Sophie, can you hear me?"

Celia's eyes snapped open. She squeezed my hands. Her pupils had become thin brown slits that split the white of her eyes down the middle.

"It's alright, I'm here," I said, my chest tight with panic.

Celia's pupils slowly returned to their normal size and shape. She stared at us as if we were strangers. "It's Faion," she said. "He's in trouble, he needs me."

She hoisted herself up onto her unsteady feet. I jumped up to wrap my arm around her for support.

"We'll find him together," I said, picking up Celia's purse.

Lily gripped my wrist. "Why are you humoring her?"

The presence of a basic around the supernatural is always a bad idea. How could I explain that I wasn't playing into the fears of an old lady and that I was, in fact, extremely worried about Faion, who was most certainly in trouble, because Celia Trice was a diviner of the highest order?

"He might be having boy trouble," I said. "She came down to see him."

Lily nodded, her concerned eyes hooked on Celia. "I'm parked right across the street," she said. "I'll drive."

Ten minutes later, Lily was pulling over outside a salmon-colored Aztec Corner apartment building on campus. I was grateful that she didn't question me when I suggested she drive on and leave us.

Celia and I climbed the stairs to the second floor. We found Faion's door unlocked. We pushed it open to find Joey in a blue bath towel kneeling over Faion's lifeless body sprawled out on the floor in an unnatural position—one of his legs folded behind him, palms facing up, his head turned away.

My heart froze. A bittersweet odor filled the room, like cinnamon mixed with cayenne pepper. Silver specks dotted the carpet all around Faion. Some of the dust had crawled onto his jeans and t-shirt.

Celia clutched her chest. I held her tight to keep her away from Faion.

I cleared my throat. "Joey, what happened?"

"Just as I turned off the shower, I heard a loud thud, like something heavy hitting the floor. I found him like this, unresponsive." He lifted his teary eyes to me. "I was in the shower too long. I was daydreaming."

I must keep it together. I need to stay strong.

"Joey, it's going to be okay," I said. "Do me a favor. Get another towel and wipe all that silver off the floor and off Faion. Every speck of it. Okay?"

His dazed look said it all. "But, I don't... You want me to clean? Isn't that evidence?"

Celia opened her purse. "Do what the girl says, dear," she told Joey. Her voice was deliberate and soothing. She quickly found a cigarette gum in her purse and unpeeled it. Her eyes lit up. "Clean all that nasty dust off my baby."

Her hypnotizing spell worked. Joey got lost in her glowing eyes like a stunned deer in the night. He rose slowly to retrieve a towel. Winter made it clear that basics weren't affected by the deadly dust. Joey would be safe.

"I have to go to my boy," Celia whispered.

"You can't and you know you can't," I whispered back. "That's silver dust. You'd end up like Faion if you get close and then you'll be no use to him."

She hung her head. Celia was on the Board of Supernatural Orders and had access to confidential information. She no doubt knew more about these scattered attacks than I did.

We both watched as the tan towel in Joey's hands sucked up the dust like it was sticky goo, leaving the towel stained in glistening silver.

"Why Faion?" Celia said, her voice clipped. "He's so young and pure-hearted. He's not a threat to anyone. Why would they do this?"

"So, the other targets have been more seasoned users of magic?"

Celia brushed off the question, instantly realizing she had already said too much. Guilt gripped me that I was the reason Faion had been targeted, as I was the reason Emmet had been kidnapped and the reason Lucia had been controlled by Chaos. I couldn't shake the feeling that everyone I cared about would suffer because of me.

Joey finished cleaning up the dust and turned to me with empty eyes.

I pointed at an old, camo backpack on the floor by Faion's desk. "Can you put the towel in that and hand it to me?"

He moved mechanically, following my orders. Celia's spell had total hold of him.

"Did you hear anything else when you were showering? Anything at all?" I asked him as I carefully took the backpack from him.

Celia snapped her fingers. Joey took a step back, startled. "I heard the door slam," he said. "A guy in a red hoodie ran past the window."

I turned to the window. There was a narrow ledge outside. The curtain was open maybe a foot and a half. How likely was it that Joey had glimpsed the perpetrator when, according to Winter, no one else ever had?

The scene replayed in my head. Had someone knocked? Did Faion open the door cheerfully and the stranger hit him with the silver dust before he even knew what was happening? Did he suffer before he lost consciousness?

Faion had been so full of life when we spoke yesterday, and now he may never speak or recognize me or Joey, or even Celia, ever again. Memories of my mother's lifeless eyes ran through me like daggers of ice. Why was this happening to Faion?

Why is everything so horrible and why is happiness such a cruel and fleeting state in this fucked-up world?

"Are we going to call an ambulance?" Joey said.

If only. Basic medicine couldn't deal with this. Nothing could, not in the Up Above, not in the Deep Down, not even in the Shadow Realm.

"Leave now," Celia said, rolling up her sleeves. "Both of you. I will take care of Faion."

Without a word, Joey grabbed his t-shirt and sweatpants from the bed and went to the bathroom.

"What about his spell?" I said.

Joey returned, dressed now, and walked right out the door.

Celia and I stared at the door as it slowly closed.

Celia nodded. "Joey will be fine. The effect will dissipate in the next hour." She sat on the floor next to Faion and stroked his forehead.

"I want to help." Each breath I took felt thin.

Celia's face was grim. "You can't. He has one chance. You need to leave, young witch. I need to try to drag my grandson back from the clutches of this curse and I need to be alone to do it. I will abuse my power and my oath to my Order, and you can't witness that."

I had to trust her. I knew that, but it was hard to leave my friend like this. Mist magic swelled in my veins—I could call on ley line energy, I could draw out devastating power from all elements, even the moon, and yet it was all useless.

I was useless. I would give all that I am, my essence, my magic, my immortality to bring back my friend. I would give my life right now, in this room, to save Faion. I knew in my bones it was my fault and I could do nothing.

Celia held her palms together inches from her closed eyes. Something cold and ancient stirred in my being. I hurried out the door and started running. Sunlight flashed into my tearful eyes. I ran blind through a blurring world and knew everything all around me was dying or already dead.

Chapter 6

Winter's red Civic approached as I stood in the lot at Trujillo's Taco Shop on the corner of Montezuma and College Ave. I walked for an hour, debating what to do, before I finally called him.

"You look like you saw a ghost," he said as I jumped into his car while he was stopped at a red light.

"It's Faion. He's..." I couldn't get any more words out. Tears ran down my cheeks. I felt sick. I hated myself. I hated everything.

Winter pulled to the curb and just looked at me. I looked at him, too. He looked airbrushed. He wore a sharp beige linen blazer over a white shirt and tight tweed pants that complimented his powerful legs. His hair was combed back. He looked cool. I must have interrupted something when I called.

His inquisitive gaze was hard to hold. "What's wrong, Luna?"

What's right? That's the real question.

"Everything," I said, yanking the backpack strap off my shoulder. "Keep this bag in the car. It's full of silver dust."

His face contorted. "You have a backpack full of silver dust?"

I shook my head. "It's a kitchen towel. Joey cleaned dust from the floor and... Faion."

He arched an eyebrow. "Your friend, the diviner?"

I wiped the tears from my cheeks. "Yes. He's been attacked, Winter. He's unresponsive."

He nodded and set his hand gently on mine. "Take me there."

The warmth of his touch shot through me. "Four blocks up, second stoplight, take a right."

"Who's this Joey?" he said.

"Faion's boyfriend. He's basic. Celia hypnotized him. It's fine. He doesn't suspect a thing."

I waited for his judgment, but he spared me. "Celia Trice is involved?"

"Yeah, she's Faion's Grandma, she's trying to reverse the damage."

"How long did you have the dust? Are you feeling anything unusual?"

"About an hour," I said. "And, no. I feel nothing."

He parked the car and studied me with interest for a moment or two, then grabbed my arm. "You're too important to take such risks."

"Blah," I said as I opened the door.

I trudged up the steps to Faion's apartment with Winter trailing.

We found Celia on the floor, right where I had left her. She sweated profusely as she hunched over Faion's lifeless body.

Her weary eyes found Winter. "Shadow Warrior," she said with a small, dry voice. "You shouldn't be here. Look what they've done to my boy."

Winter scanned the room with the prowling eyes of a predator. "Foolish witches," he said, pointing at a silver spot in the corner which Joey had missed. "Dumb luck is the only reason you're not in vegetative states yourselves."

"Miss Celia is not a witch," I protested.

With a flick of his wrist, he threw a force field around the dust which made it swell, then contract, then swell again with a loud popping sound to double the size.

"It's rising like bread in the oven," I said, flabbergasted. "Can't you just destroy it? You know, vaporize it or something?"

"Not while its molecular structure is unstable and unknown."

I dropped to my knees and took Celia's hand. "How's he doing?"

She shook her head. "It's impenetrable. There's no way to sneak past the spell. His memories are lost."

A word hung in my throat. "Is it... necromancy?"

Winter's blue eyes shimmered. "Why would you ask that?"

"Why not? Hasn't the thought crossed your mind?"

I helped Celia climb to her feet. "A ritualistic force drives this dust spell," she said. "I can't influence it at all. Every time I try to crack through its surface, I'm slammed back by my own power. It's like punching a rubber wall."

Winter reached down and gently picked up Faion.

"Is it safe to move him?" I said.

He laid Faion on the bed and then stood there. "Nothing can disturb him now."

Celia sat on the bed and I sat next to her. She lifted Faion's head and placed it on a pillow. Her gaze was empty. Her steely resolve had seemingly vanished. "How will I tell his mother?" she muttered.

I swallowed down a sob. She may never speak to him again. No one should ever have to survive their own grandchildren.

Winter was hard to read. Thoughts streamed through his eyes in rapid succession. "Anything else?" he said.

"Joey saw someone," I blurted out.

Winter leaned back against the wall. "Where's this Joey now?"

Strange. He didn't seem surprised the attacker had slipped up.

Celia placed Faion's arms by his sides. "The etheric residue of my hypnotizing spell will persist on Joey for a while. It will guide me to his location."

She sat with perfect posture and her hands on her thighs. She closed her eyes and breathed in slowly, searching for magic echoes on Joey.

Winter got down on his knees. He studied the spot where Faion had been found. He held his hand just above the carpet. "Here. Can you sense it?"

"I'm sorry," I said. "Sense what?"

He brought his fingers to his nose, sniffing. "Ambient dissonance, a kind of pervasive magic yet reverberating. The assailant never bothered to mask the etheric energy."

The ever-careful dark entity suddenly turning reckless? Why?

"He's there," Celia said with urgency. "My spell still hovers over him, warming his innocent soul like a soft blanket."

The very sound of the word *innocent* almost hurt right now. "Where?"

"There's a brick path. He's sitting there."

"Aztec Walk," I said. "It's minutes away."

"I'll try to reactivate the spell, it could guide him to us," Celia said.

"Nah. No need. I got this."

We had messed with Joey's head enough. Faion wouldn't approve. I ran out the door and down a side street to the start of Aztec Walk. Joey was sitting right in the middle of the path. Students jogged and walked around him like he was a permanent monument.

"Hey, Joey," I said with tenderness. "Take my hand."

He rose suddenly without expression and took my hand. I turned around and led him back down the street to Faion's apartment.

When we walked through the door, Joey spotted Winter and stopped cold.

The Immortal brute's face had the unblinking intensity of a Grizzly bear, his eyes glistening with savage, concentrated violence.

What the hell? Was his plan really to terrify the witness?

I elbowed Winter, then walked to Joey. "Please, he's harmless. His face is just stuck on heartless asshole. We need to ask you a few questions."

"Didn't I tell you before?" Joey paused, unsure of his own memory.

"You did, yeah," I said, "but when you got that glimpse of the man, did you see his face, his eyes, anything like that?"

Joey took a moment. "I don't think... no, it all happened so fast."

"He saw the man's face," Winter said, drily.

I shot him a scolding look. "How would you even know that?" I returned my attention to Joey. "Maybe close your eyes. In that flash of a second, was there a skin tone or jawline or a marking? Faion's life may depend on it."

The mention of Faion's name gave Joey a jolt. "Wait, why is Faion still here? Why's he not at the hospital? Something's not right. Something's off about all of you. Why did I leave here before? My mind's playing tricks."

"It's tough on all of us," I said. "We're all out of sorts right now." I grabbed a notebook from a counter and flipped to a blank page to tear it out. "Faion said you're an artist. Could you sketch the suspect?"

He pushed past me and marched to the bed. "You're all crazy, we're taking Faion to a hospital!"

With a grunt, Winter snatched the notebook from my hands and gave me a dismissive glare. "Enough," he said, then held his right arm out to the side and pointed his fingers at Joey who was instantly frozen inside a translucent force field. His arms and legs began to spasm as his body slowly levitated.

Blue light sparked from Winter's fingers, forming a funnel shape as it elongated toward Joey's face. He held the notebook open with his free hand.

Joey blinked a few times, blinded by the light, suspended in the air, arms dangling at his sides. His whole body writhed as a thin orange beam emerged from the funnel of light to target his forehead. The blue light swung around and rushed toward Winter in a swirl of threadlike rays.

The threads hit the notebook page like a bundle of fine needles, thumbing out gray lines and curves on the paper in a brisk, embroidery pattern, like a sewing machine.

Then, as if a switch had been turned off, the light beams dissolved into a spiraling mist that disappeared before reaching the floor.

Celia shook her head. "You do that so easily. I don't

understand. Not even the strongest among the seers and diviners can retrace memories embedded in the deep subconscious without losing consciousness and passing out."

Winter released the force field that held Joey in place until the young man landed roughly on his feet. Joey hugged himself like a lost little child.

I moved closer to Winter to get a better look at the full color sketch in the notebook that had been extracted directly from Joey's unconscious.

The face of a young man in his mid-twenties stared at me with wide open brown eyes. He looked surprised, like a child caught stealing from a cookie jar. A few curly strands of brown hair peeked from under a red hoodie. A sparse goatee traced his chin. His nose was wide and crooked as if it had been broken and poorly healed. His lips were pursed.

The precision of the drawing took me aback. It put police sketches to shame. I wanted to reach out to see if it was flesh.

"That's strange," Winter said.

"It's been strange for a while," I said under my breath.

Winter looked to Celia. "Ms. Trice, please make sure this young man forgets he ever saw me. He must have no recollection of what transpired."

Celia nodded. "I will guide him to the heart of campus."

"I trust you'll be transporting your grandson to the under realm?"

"One does what one must." Celia raised her eyes to Winter. "You may have days where your undying might seem a curse, but at very least it has spared you the grievous agony of losing a beloved child."

Winter's face hardened as he fought back dark impulses.

I wished a chronomaster was nearby so I could make him reverse time. I knew Celia's words had unintentionally awoke Winter's greatest heartache, chasing his thoughts back to 1955 when he had lost his one and only child, a little boy named Christian, born to a mortal mother. His devastation was so complete it had alarmed even the Grand Magistrate, Düsternis. I had decided to never tell Winter I had read about it in the Eternal Archives at the Sacred Vault before Chaos set the whole place ablaze.

Winter exhaled through his nose. "I'll leave it to your hands," he said and walked out the door.

I lay my hand on Celia's shoulder. "We'll bring Faion back. I promise."

Promises were often the last breath of desperation, but I vowed that this promise would not ring hollow. I intended to move heaven and earth to bring Faion back to us.

Outside, Winter turned and grabbed my forearm. I recoiled. His skin burned unnaturally hot and his grip was anything but tender.

"Joey was not the only witness," he said, his voice assuming its usual harsh authority. "There was another attack on campus earlier today."

Of course, because wherever I go, also goes heinous bullshit.

"My god," I said with defeat. "And they saw the red hoodie guy?"

"Yes and no."

"You're going to have to choose one."

Winter took a piece of paper from his jacket pocket. As he unfolded it, I began to see the penciled portrait of a man with near identical features to the man in the red hoodie—same brown eyes, same curly hair, same goatee, same misshapen nose. There was only one major difference. The man in this new drawing was clearly older, probably thirty years older, in his mid-fifties, and yet I was immediately convinced it was the same man.

"You think it's him, too," Winter said.

I nodded. "Yeah, it's absolutely him and now I know what it feels like to lose my mind."

Winter narrowed his eyes. "Unless it's not anyone."

I had no choice but to humor him. "Not anyone... care to explain?"

"I can't," he said.

"You can't? Great. Now we're both losing it," I said and then studied the sketch again. "Two witnesses on the same day? It's like they stopped caring."

"They care," he said. "This is by design, Luna. It's phase two—the provocation phase."

"That's not a thing," I said. "You made that up. You just said it's not anyone, and now your non-entity has a bunch of cheesy phases."

Winter's phone buzzed before he had a chance to explain. As he read the message on the screen, his face turned dark. I braced myself for bad news.

"Now three witnesses," he said. "This one near Lincoln Park. A sea witch claims to have seen an elderly man escape the scene. I bet if we saw his face, we'd recognize it despite the wrinkles."

You're middle-aged, you're young, you're old... which way are you going, Benjamin Button?

Winter opened the door of his Civic. "I need to get to the lab. I want to compare this new silver dust sample with the others. Want to come along?"

I shook my head. "I'm no help at all in a lab, and I have to call Gram. How about we hook up later? You know, meet up and compare notes."

Hook up? I should never talk.

"Very well," he said. "Want me to drop you somewhere?"

"I need to clear my head. I'll walk. It's not that far."

Winter took my hand before I could turn to go. "I appreciate what you've been through, Luna. I am not without feeling."

"Good to know," I said as my heart began to accelerate. Now his hand was the perfect temperature and it soothed me all the way to my center.

"When this is done, I'll tell you things," he said as he released my hand and sat in his Civic.

"Things? How about answers?"

"Yeah, I have answers, but I don't have all of them." He started his car and revved the engine. "Some questions only Chaos can answer."

His eyes flashed up at mine.

"I'm tired of all these Immortal games," I said. "Really, I am. You all wield your secrets like petty despots."

Winter laughed. "I've missed you, Miss Collinsworth."

He drove off, grinning stupidly inside his dingy little ride.

Chapter 7

MESSING WITH MY HEAD was kind of Winter's thing. Instead of walking off my frantic thoughts and achieving some semblance of mental and emotional stability, all I could think about was the carrot he had dangled about my past.

As I neared the steps to the library, a sparkly mound on top of a stone flowerbed caught my eye. My heart slowed down with recognition.

Son of a bitch. The shiny pile was made of silver dust—sparkling, breathing, swelling dust. I quickly protected myself with an invisible energy shield.

I looked about before I summoned a blue force field into my palm. I had to be swift. My mist magic was barely detectable by orbs, diviners and even the Eternals themselves, but basics could still see it if they happened by.

I hurled the blue field forward to entrap the dust within a crystalized sphere. The dust hissed and sizzled as it ricocheted all over the place inside the energy sphere.

What in the world? Is that stuff alive?

None of my senses reacted to any unknown stimuli. There was no strange scratching at my etheric essence as Winter had described it. Maybe mist riders were immune to the damn thing, but that wasn't a bet I was willing to take.

Something had to be done about an active pile of deadly dust in the middle of the campus, but what? I couldn't very well call Waste Management and request a removal of toxic materials.

Whether I liked it or not, I had to ask Winter for help.

As far as habits go, this was becoming a bad one.

I scrolled for his number on my phone.

A bloodcurdling growl stopped me in my tracks. The hairs on my neck bristled. Remembering to breathe, I spun around.

A towering demonic beast glared at me through button-like eyes that were black as coal. The left eye protruded a little from its socket as if hanging by a ligament. Green slobber dripped down its hide, forming uneven bumps that swelled, then melted into nothingness before more green slobber dripped down and the gruesome process repeated. The beast's misshapen snout and drooling fangs emitted a horrific, foul odor.

Two more beasts appeared behind the first one, equally rank and disgusting, staring through me with their coal button eyes.

Stepping back, heart thumping, I noticed two cyclists

rounding a corner in the distance, pedaling our way. I had to act fast.

I called the elements around me to enter my bloodstream and flood me with pure energy. The magic current pulsed in my fingertips, as I readied to let loose. I marched at the fiends until I bumped hard against an invisible wall.

The world went black. A complete and utter darkness swallowed up everything, like the sun and the moon and the stars had burned out. I did not feel blind, I felt suspended in a void.

A great whooshing hum cut through the void, first startling me, then shooting me upwards. Now I was caught in a spinning whirlwind. My stomach lunged and I struggled to hold its contents. The French toast and mint chocolate shake I had for lunch burned my throat.

Eat crap and face the consequences. Will I ever learn?

Over and over, I slammed against confinements I couldn't see. I was tearing at the seams, cells colliding, molecules stretching as if some force was trying to separate my soul from my body. Then it stopped. I fell to my hands and knees.

Gradually, the void faded to a dark limbo where my eyes could see burning white silhouettes of the monsters standing a few yards away.

I was trapped in a warped time vortex. My heart was in my throat. I had studied this at school for like two days. I never imagined this was still a thing or that I, of all people, would ever be stuck in it.

Think, think, think.

I shuffled through faint training memories like a deck of cards. The only way out of this would be to slaughter the beasts and extract their essence. Only then could I escape the vortex walls. That was the theory anyway. Too bad I could not remember a single detail of that magic.

All I knew was that failure meant I'd be trapped in this timelessness, alone and starving, unable even to die, just stranded for eternity, battling these foul monsters in an endless loop of panic and agony.

The monsters roared with a grating, primal force. Gray drool dripped from their fangs to mix with the green slobber that slid all over their wet, patchy hides.

So beyond gross.

They charged as one. Their bodies jiggled almost like gelatin. With no elemental sources at hand and all access to ley lines cut off, the only energy I could channel was what was stored inside my magic core. The question was, how much magic did I have left before my tank would run dry?

With a primal roar of my own, I built up a wall of green energy that knocked those furry Jell-O monsters back. All three tumbled to the ground, but a second later bounded up to come at me from three different directions.

They learn quick. That's unfortunate.

Gathering a substantial amount of my core energy, I spun a shimmering shield around me to brace for the oncoming assault.

The beasts attacked at dizzying speeds, their gaping maws and shining fangs readying to rip into my soft flesh.

The first leapt at me, snarling like a demon hound from hell. I crouched and the beast flew right over me, searing its belly on the blazing current of my sizzling shield. Smoke and yellow puss poured from its charred underside and the foulest stench hit my nostrils, gagging me.

The other two monsters were in the air.

I fed more magic into my force field. One of the beasts twirled away right before colliding with my shield. The third beast landed on the shield with a spine-chilling howl. A massive paw cut through the force field, its huge claws swiping at my left arm, gashing open the flesh from shoulder to elbow, shredding muscles and tendons alike.

Excruciating pain shot through me like a hot iron spike. *What the hell?* The beasts could penetrate my best shield, and my core was weakening as fast as it was spilling out the last of my energy.

I'm immortal, how could my end have come so fast?

The injured beast joined the other two. It had already completely healed. All three glared as blood drenched my skin and clothes. If I used my energy for regeneration, I'd have nothing left to fight them off.

I spun around and hurled balls of energy blindly. One of them hit a beast in the gut, burning straight through flesh and organs, leaving a grapefruit-sized hole in its wake. The beast went down, arms and legs quaking for a moment before it stopped moving. One dead, two to go.

The surviving beasts snarled, baring their teeth. They must have known they couldn't kill me. Their mission was to keep me in the warped time vortex for as long as they could. Serious shit must be happening on the outside and I couldn't do a single thing to help.

My kingdom for a sword.

Wait. Not a sword in sight, but maybe, just maybe... an ice spear.

I had to be all in on this gamble. I let the shield fizzle out and I charged the beasts, screaming. I'd needed to extract every unneeded drop of moisture in my skin and eyes and off the hides of those slippery monsters to summon enough water energy to fill my empty hands with an ice spear.

They leapt at me, drooling and unafraid. Their jaws shifted and opened wide enough to swallow my whole skull. This was the world's worst idea until my grip cooled and I thrust my brand-new ice spear toward the belly of a beast, but both beasts suddenly just disappeared.

Oh, come on, really?

Claws slashed through my back, scraping off fabric and skin. I howled from the stinging pain. Grinding my teeth, I swirled around, raging. Mist oozed out of my fingers in clumps and enveloped my hands and arms. Elation filled my lungs as my injured arm healed.

Power rose within me like a colossal tidal wave. I drove my bare hand deep into the green slushy mess that was the monster's chest, slicing through wet membranes, cartilage and sticky flesh, puncturing the heart. The beast's blood drenched my hand and arm, hot and putrid.

Astonished, I watched the beast collapse to the ground, lifeless. I had no idea where all that power had come from. In my gut, I knew it was mist magic, but I didn't know how I had accessed it or how to do it again.

I bent down and grabbed the dead beast by the arm. I swung it around my head and hurled it at the last monster who retreated, growling through a mess of rotten teeth.

The beast shuffled back and forth, uncertain what to do next. The mist in my hands formed an electric whip that leapt forward and wrapped around the creature's throat. I yanked the ugly motherfucker close so I could point my fingers at its dark eyes and extract its wicked essence, the same way Winter had done to Dimitri.

Whatever Shadow Warriors do, Mist Riders do better.

"You're coming with me, buddy," I told the beast. "I need to find out exactly what you are."

The creature opened its hideous mouth, but no voice came out. Steam started bubbling where its eyes had been. I felt its etheric essence for an instant like sharpened glass on my skin, awful, unsettling like the most frantic nightmare. Then the beast's legs gave in as if being sucked into the ground.

The two dead bodies followed suit, folding onto themselves and then all three beasts shriveled to dust and melted out of existence. A warm breeze dispersed the dust. Suddenly, all oxygen was gone. My lungs burned. The vortex spun out of control and me with it. I fell into a vacuum. My heart fluttered. The vortex disintegrated and I was left standing on the stairs outside the library, panting in the bright California sun.

There was no sign of the beasts. When I looked down at my left arm, the sleeve of my blouse had been torn open, the only proof of my dark battle.

Chapter 8

"Dude, I've seen some total bizarro bullshit since I met you, but those hideous slobber beasts were the legit most heinous, most hideous, most preposterous abominations I have ever come across. Like ever."

Winter shook a test tube vigorously. "Welcome to the wild side of life, all part of life's rich pageant."

He was barely listening. His so-called lab wasn't what you would call state-of-the-art. It consisted of a large desk with a microscope and two glass cabinets with test tubes, droppers, brushes and scales. It had been set up in Winter's *super special secret room* as Faion had dubbed it. This was the same room where Winter had hacked into the Seventh Council's database to hunt for clues about the soul swallowers who had burglarized my apartment and kidnapped Emmet.

This time the place was less tidy—papers and books were stacked everywhere, and a balled-up blanket on the loveseat meant Winter had probably spent the night here.

"Did you hear what I said?" I insisted. "I was almost entombed in a time vortex forever, screaming and pulling my hair out in a claustrophobic torture chamber battling against hideous... Never mind, you're clearly not interested in the fact that I'll probably have permanent terror in my psyche now and never be able to go in my closet again."

"I'm listening," he said in the way that men think they're listening because they *heard* the words, but they weren't listening because they didn't *feel* the words.

"Yeah, with man ears, I get it."

"So, you get a walk-in closet," he said.

"Do you want to die right now?"

"If only."

If I'm being honest, the banter helped.

"What are you doing?" I said to change the subject. "When did you become a chemist exactly? Did you study with Victor Frankenstein?"

"I did visit the University of Ingolstadt in Bavaria in the late 18th century, but I did not run into any fictional characters while on campus."

That was such a fanboy comment. I pretended to get it.

Using a dropper, Winter emptied some of the test tube contents onto a glass microscope slide and slowly lowered a glass cover slip over the sample to keep it in place, then reached out for my hand to pull me close.

"Check this out," he said, mounting the slide onto the microscope. "Look right here. What do you see?"

I peeked into the eyepiece. "What should I be seeing?"

There was nothing like the kaleidoscope cell patterns I expected. Instead, I made out a landscape of mountain snowcaps and cotton candy clouds. It felt odd and shocking and a somehow appropriate part of my day from hell.

"Silver dust," he said. "I've stabilized it using a chemical agent developed in the 17th century by Van Helmont, an Immortal alchemist. It traces and illuminates magic reverberations."

"Alchemy? That's not a thing," I scoffed.

"Not to mortals, but we're also not a thing to mortals."

What? "No. I call bullshit. I've studied both basic and supernatural history. Alchemy is not real in either world. It's not science or magic."

He tried to hold back a satisfied smile, but a little bit sneaked out.

"The girl who found out she's a living myth, a mist rider no less, is now having problems believing other supernatural revelations?"

"Alchemy? *Really?*"

He finally unleashed his satisfied grin. "Messing with you, mist rider. Van Helmont did legitimate science as well. This had nothing to do with melting metals down to turn them into gold or his search for the philosopher's stone."

"You're a complete bother," I said.

"Yeah, so I've been told. Van Helmont further developed this centuries later, back in the late 1950s, as part of a larger contingency plan to decode sources of magic and witchcraft. He was trying to find a way to control the users, your fellow Deep Downers."

My utter contempt for Immortals must have been obvious.

"Hey, don't look at me. I never liked him, and it clearly didn't work. However, I've discovered that his work is highly effective when working with volatile compounds such as this silver reactive substance."

He directed my attention back to the microscope. My eyes widened as I took a glance. The specimen puffed and pulsated, stretching, spreading until the image blurred.

"My god, it's constantly multiplying," I said. "You'd only need to disperse a tiny amount of that to cause huge damage."

A little bit could take out the entire Deep Down.

Winter switched off the microscope light, retrieved the slide, carefully placed it inside a small titanium box and locked it. "It behaves organically, contracting or expanding as it reacts to external stimuli."

Awe and terror ran in my veins. "You don't mean it's sentient?"

Winter's eyebrows came together. "Not quite, more like an amoeba carrying an embedded code in its core, a code that initiates behavior and effectively weaponizes the dust to adapt to new environments. The speed at which it adapts makes it appear sensory and instinctive."

"That's a nice trick," I said. "It's technology, not magic."

"Technology is mind magic," he said. "Even humans can practice it."

"How do you explain how the slobber monsters turned into dust? There has to be a connection, right?"

He shrugged. "Connection is a word with a thousand meanings. The only thing I can tell you is that those creatures were not alive."

"Not alive? If they were dead, they really sucked at it."

He brightened. "Think of them as zombies."

"*Zombies? Alchemists?* Jonas, you need to get some sleep."

I apparently amused him. "Thought that would be an easy reference for you and your Gen Z brain. What I mean is undead. They were once alive, then died, then were brought back in a degraded, easily controlled form."

"What? Remote-control zombies?"

He straightened his desk. "The warped time vortex that grabbed you, it's a necromantic apparatus."

Right. It had been said that Necromancers commanded entire armies of dead in ancient times. With those armies, they had fought alongside and against Immortals, always choosing the winning side. I had recurring nightmares about them as a kid.

I decided to come clean. "I spoke with a seer."

He stared at me. "You mean Penelope Osvaldo? I know."

Wait, what?

"How the hell do you know?"

He switched off the lights in the lab and led me to the next room.

"You told me."

"I didn't tell you. I didn't tell anyone."

"When humans speak, it's always a confession," he said. "You blatantly told me that someone was going to fill you in on your familial relationship to Chaos. It took about two minutes of digging to discover which seers often crossed paths with Celia Trice."

"I am not a human," I said.

"Your naïve approach to... well, everything, is all too human."

"Damn it, Jonas! You can't just co-opt my life whenever you want."

"Seemed like you wanted me to know."

"I didn't," I yelled. "You're infuriating. You used your web of creeps to invade every bit of my privacy."

"That's done," he said, waving his hand dismissively. "The seer, what did she see?"

"She said my mother was under a necromantic spell."

His blue eyes darkened. "Did she?"

"Come on, spit it out. What's in your head?" I insisted.

"It's likely an Eternal was involved. Both then and now."

If an Eternal attacked my mother and me, how did we even survive?

Winter drank spring water from a bottle. "You're probably wondering how you survived an Eternal attack."

"I survived because that's what *Horror* wanted."

"Slow down. We don't know it was Horror. He would have been secretly amassing power for decades under the Eternals' noses. That's not likely."

"Likely? Unlikely? Those words have lost all meaning to me."

"That's fair, but Eternals have allied with necromancers since the dawn of time to achieve their objectives. It could be any of them."

"Could be, yet you don't sound convinced."

He dunked the empty water bottle in the trash. "There's a theory, a rumor really, that the darkest necromantic magic always traces back to Horror."

"When I said it was Horror, you told me to slow down."

"It's a theory. We need to consider everything," he said.

"Tell me this theory."

He tore open a PowerBar and took a bite. "Okay, so, the necromancers had this ability," he said while chewing. He stopped to swallow. "They had the ability to communicate with the recently departed and access memories still imprinted in brain cells, but they couldn't command the dead or even prolong the transitory state between life and death. The theory goes that it was Horror himself who bestowed that power upon them."

"Sounds like he owns their asses," I concluded.

"Like I said, it's a theory."

I grabbed his arm. "And I'm the reason for it all, the attack on my mother *and* the current attacks. Chaos may have fooled Düsternis when he took the blame for the slaughter and the fire at the Sacred Vault, but Horror would have seen right through it. He knows what I am or, at very least, suspects it. How am I doing? How aH"

Winter's eyes looked tired. "Before you go further, I can tell you with certainty that Düsternis is not involved. Not this time. There's been an undeclared war between the Seventh Council and the Necro Order since a Chief Necromancer betrayed Düsternis while they conspired together to limit the power of the Eternals over Immortal Councils. Düsternis was stripped of his authority for more than a century. There's no way he'd ever make another pact with the necromancers."

Shit. The Horror show was about to begin. *There's no stopping it now.* He was coming and he'd be bringing his morbid apprentices, no Immortal mediators like Düsternis needed this time.

I struggled to breathe. "How about the other Eternals? Can't they be warned? Maybe they'll be able to do something?"

"It would have to come from someone they trust."

I had gravely offended Horror. I thwarted his plans at the Sacred Vault the first time he came for me. Unlike Düsternis, Horror had nothing to lose and everything to gain. He would never stop hunting me.

As much as I hated to admit it, I needed Chaos like

yesterday. He had insight into Horror's sick head, and he was my only possible ally who also carried part of Horror's immeasurable powers.

"Someone they trust?" I said in a daze. "Who do Eternals trust?"

I covered my face with both hands. My fate had been sealed since birth because of my doomed genes and I had probably been leaving a trail of my scent everywhere for Horror to follow. I could accept that. I was willing to pay whatever price to appease the universe, but Faion should not have suffered because of my evil ancestors and whatever crimes I was sure they had committed throughout time.

Winter was silent. Something like pity lingered in his eyes.

He readied to speak when someone knocked on the door twice—a gentle, short *tap tap* like a late-night lover tapping on a windowpane.

A moment later, Kirsi, Immortal warrior, guard of the Seventh Council Seal and ready-to-ride Valkyrie strolled in, tall and slim, dressed in black leather jacket and faded jeans, brown hair pulled back into a ponytail, sword sheathed on her back as if poised for battle.

The last time I saw her, she had invited me to join the Society of Immortal Sisterhood and Order of Peace Fighters and I had almost accepted, but then I spent hours wondering why I was invited in the first place. Considering Kirsi and Winter were BFFs, how many of my secrets had he revealed to her?

Winter looked relieved to see her. "What did you find?"

"The noise originates from..." Kirsi paused when she spotted me.

Good. He hasn't told her everything.

Winter gestured her to continue.

"It's coming from the south equinoctial observatory," she said.

"The south equinoctial observatory?" I repeated.

"Yeah," Kirsi said. "Echoes and reverberations are leaking out."

"I understood none of that," I confessed.

"It's one of the three main portals to the Eternal Halls, located on the very tip of the Tierra del Fuego archipelago," Winter explained. "Eternal portals are supposed to be deadly quiet."

"But they're not quiet," I said. "What does that mean?"

"It means we're all fucked," Kirsi said. "Excuse my French."

Winter grabbed his car keys. "Ladies, show yourselves out."

"Wait, where are you going?" I said, but he was already out the door.

Whatever. I'm tired of arguing with him.

Kirsi set her sword on the counter, then plopped onto the loveseat. "Good to see you two have put your personal differences aside."

Is it? Have we?

I shrugged. Personal differences and hurt feelings seemed so last week. People were hit with deadly necromancy and Eternal portals were leaking magic. "You think he's headed to that leaky observatory?"

She arched an eyebrow. "What do you think?"

I doubted either of us really knew. "I assume he's walking straight into the fires of hell."

Kirsi chuckled. "Sounds about right."

"I take it you know all about the whole silver dust thing."

She nodded. "Came back from Europe as soon as he called."

"Did he mention that your council doesn't want to help?"

"He didn't have to, Luna. I long ago gave up on the council acting with unselfish valor. They're a patriarchal, myopic sect paralyzed by analysis. Been that way since Düsternis took the reins. I'm about the Sisterhood now."

"The Sisterhood of the cakes," I said. "That's growing on me."

Kirsi smiled, then became suddenly serious. "erI heard about your friend." She reached up to squeeze my hand. "For what it's worth, Winter will dig and rip his way through the underworld and chop off the head of the Devil himself to make this right. And we'll help him."

An unexpected pang of regret crept up inside my chest. "I may not have told you this before, Kirsi, but I'm grateful we've become friends."

"Cool," she said. "I feel the same, but are we the kind

of friends who can order a pizza together? I've been on the move all day."

"Sure," I said. "Okay, we have to eat."

"Perfect. And let's use the big guy's credit card," she said with a wink.

Chapter 9

TAM'S EYES BEAMED LIKE enchanted gems. Her hug was way too tight but welcome. The value of a true friend in dark times is immeasurable.

"You are a sight for sore eyes, Tam."

"In times of war," she said, "I'll never be far."

Her spiky brown pixie hair seemed to reflect her restless etheric essence. I had never seen Tam so uneasy before. She had traveled all the way down from Palomar Mountain where the mother portal to the Deep Down lay beneath a giant incense cedar.

Tam couldn't travel via the kinetic forces of the ley lines like Winter and I could. The Lunar Order had forbidden its witches from accessing such raw, unrefined energy that could shred most users of magic to pieces. She had to use basic transportation, which meant it took her two hours to get to the secluded Solana Beach, twenty miles north of San Diego, to sit with me at a picnic table overlooking the surf.

I didn't like that she had made the trip on her own, not with all the silver dust attacks, but then again Tam Nguyen was no ordinary witch. She wielded magic like a virtuoso, and she had reflexes and instincts like a jungle cat.

"Any news of Faion?" I asked her.

"Resting comfortably," she said.

I turned and saw waves breaking on the shore. *Resting comfortably*. How many times had I heard those reassuring words about my mother when I was a girl? I was never once reassured.

I hadn't slept last night. Panic and uncertainty coursed through me, then and now. My world was tilting off its axis. One saving grace was that Gram had agreed to stay put in Astoria. I told her I had a few college things to do before I would hurry home to see her. The fact that she didn't mention silver dust gave me hope that the attacks hadn't yet reached Oregon.

Tam narrowed her eyes. "The GC called an emergency meeting of all leaders of all magic Orders and supernatural factions on the West Coast."

"The Great Chanter himself?"

"Yeah, Horpheus summoned everyone," Tam said. "It was a sight to behold. All, and I mean all, of the Deep Down's finest were there as well as the revered and exalted expats who live in the outer lands above. Your world."

Horpheus was a seasoned mage who excelled at chants, incantations and magic charms. He was the Region's first-in-command, the Great Chanter, and all factions and orders of the West answered to him. Unlike a leader like Düsternis who reeked of privilege and arrogance, his authority had been hard earned, steady and well deserved.

I struggled to accept Tam's words. "All the exalted and revered of all the outside factions?"

If that was the case, it could mean only one thing.

She grinned. "Luna, it was crazy. There were troglodytes, forest mages, druids, northern fae, you name it, spirit beings and even some notorious banished sorcerers who practice outlawed ancient magic. Okay, maybe one invitation did get lost in the mail, the shapeshifters."

That made sense. The rare times shifters had been allowed inside the Deep Down, they immediately caused political and social upheaval. In their culture, it was highly valued to be impulsive, belligerent and scheming. Emmet was an exception as he had grown up half-blooded and shaped largely by the culture of his human half.

"Faion was the straw that broke the camel's back?"

Tam bent her face, playing back my words in her head. "If you're asking me if Faion's attack was the reason for the meeting, then yes. Celia is high up in the Region's Divining Order and when her grandson met the same fate as the other unfortunate souls, the magic realm took notice."

"By now all charmed folk must know about the attacks."

"Unless they are living under a rock or off the grid, they know about the silver dust attacks," Tam said. Her penetrating gaze lost its usual edge.

"All that innocence lost," I added.

Tam raised her hand to fiddle her fingers in a sea breeze. The incoming wave reacted to her magic, soaring fifteen feet high before dispersing into a thousand translucent bubbles. A misty spray leapt from the ocean and raced towards us, cooling our skin with the tickling touch of sea vapor.

"Tam, can you deliver a message for me?"

"I'm here to help, Luna, whatever you need."

"That means a lot," I said. I took a moment to clear my mind. "Please, tell Celia that we have confirmation that necromancers are involved as well as..." My heartbeat accelerated. "It's more than likely the necromancers are taking their orders from someone in the Eternal Halls."

Tam struggled to process this new information. "An Eternal?" She stared through me as I nodded. "What would the Eternals be hoping to gain? If the magic world were wholly eradicated, who would they rule over? They're the wise ones, right? Petty human politics hold no interest to them."

Wise ones my ass.

I decided not to tell Tam that the Eternal pulling the strings might well be Horror, the vicious disruptor, bent on revenge, nor would I tell her that he was trying to smoke out a mist rider, the first born in a thousand years.

I shrugged. "All I know is the world's gone mad."

A light dawned in Tam. "That would mean that when necromancers were trying to recruit elite troglodyte forces last year, it was on an Eternal's orders."

"Your guess is as good as mine," I said.

"No, my guess is better," she said. "That's exactly what happened."

I had fought against troglodytes and a dwarf legion at the Sacred Vault. Their reactions were sluggish, their spirits subdued—in the end, when Chaos made them submit to his will, they regressed into an infantile state.

Tam's realization made it clear that Horror's plan had been in motion for quite some time. Those poor souls had been dragged back to life from a brain-dead state by Horror's sinister wielders of dark magic. Killing them was not an act of violence, it was an act of kindness.

My phone buzzed. It was a text from Emmet.

> *need to talk ASAP Lily said u r back please call*

Lily told me she had seen Emmet, but I became distracted when Celia entered a trance. After all hell broke loose with Faion, I never got a chance to ask Lily for the details.

I handed Tam a sealed envelope. "Give this to Celia. She'll know what to do with it."

Tam creased her forehead. "What's this?"

"Evidence we've collected on the silver dust."

"*We?*"

"I need you to trust me, okay?" I said, ignoring her question. "There are microscopic images of the dust in there. It responds to magic stimuli and it expands. If Horpheus and the Board don't know, they need to know."

Tam's voice held a touch of reproach. "I trust you, Luna, but the question seems to be, do you trust me? I don't know where you get all your information and I won't ask. Maybe someday you'll trust me enough to say."

I gave her a hug, feeling guilty but revealing nothing.

EMMET'S BACHELOR PAD WAS what you would expect for someone as busy and driven as Emmet: lean in décor, neutral in colors, untidy yet clean. Despite having dated this man, I had never been inside his apartment.

His prolonged hug at the door possessed the gentlest strength. His hazel eyes brimmed with positivity. He had become even more attractive since I last saw him—tanned, toned and glowing with health. I felt a bittersweet pang of nostalgia. Emmet was the last chapter of my life before I learned what I was.

"It's so good to see you, Sophie," he said as he let go. "I wondered if we'd ever see each other again."

"It's good to see you, too," I said. I decided to get right to the chase. "You and Lily, you've met up?"

A glimmer of guilt darkened his eyes. "Yeah, we did, I hope you don't mind, we met a few times."

A few times? Lily failed to mention that.

I shrugged. "Hey, you don't need my permission. I assume every man wants to hang with Lily. She's smart. She's gorgeous. I get it."

He looked offended. "Wow. Are you being serious right now? You honestly believe I asked you over to tell you I was dating your best friend?"

Uh-oh, I swallowed a bug. "Nothing would surprise me."

"Well, you surprise me," he said. "Not everyone is out to get you, Sophie. You know that Lily wouldn't do that. And you should know I wouldn't do that."

"I'm just saying it's none of my business."

He shook his head. "We met to talk about you. We both missed you. The first time, we just talked about how you were doing over there. The second time, I asked for your Swedish phone number. She shut me down, told me you'd be back for Easter."

I smiled. "Lily shuts people down. She's a badass."

"She's definitely not a person to trifle with."

"Okay, so what's up, Emmet? Meeting me comes with risks, I think you know that."

He knew. The last time we met he nearly died in the dungeons of the Sacred Vault. After that, he was wise enough to keep his distance. It hurt a little that he never broke down and called, but it was for the best.

Something has changed his mind.

"This isn't about us," he said, pursing his lips. "I know our chance has passed. Someone wants to meet you, an important person."

That I did not expect. "You're a matchmaker now?"

"Sophie, this isn't a joke."

Something in his low, guttural tone alarmed me.

"Fine, okay, who?" I said.

"Cyrus McDonnell."

I licked my lips. "Should that name mean something to me?"

"I thought maybe, but he's the Higher Alpha of the local pack."

Oh boy. Shifters. I might not have heard of Cyrus McDonnell, but I had heard quite a few cautionary tales about pack leaders in general.

"How do I swipe left?" I said. "Emmet, do I have to? My plate is overfull with Immortals and necromancers and microscopes. I don't need to add hotheaded, alpha howlers to my plate."

"*Howlers?* Play nice, okay? I'm aware you're dealing with a lot. So is Cyrus. That's why he wants to talk to you."

I fixed my eyes on him. "How does he even know of me?"

"Cyrus has heard rumors. He knows every supernatural faction, even the banished and the rogue, have been invited down to the under realms. These attacks are happening in his territory. He wants a seat at that table with the Board of Supernatural Orders. He needs a connective link."

The truth started to dawn on me. "Oh shit, *I'm* the matchmaker?"

"Yeah, you're his one and only candidate."

"And by not answering my question about how Cyrus would even know of me, I can assume you told him."

Emmet sat back in his chair and flared his nostrils. "I had no choice."

"No choice? That's a weak response. You're buddies with the pack leader now? And here I thought you were a lone wolf."

"Whether official or not, all shifters are instinct bound to the pack."

Wishy washy BS.

"Well, dude, you gave your pack daddy some bad intel. They didn't invite me to their table either. I'm not privy to all that, nor have I been to the Deep Down since I've been home. They basically give zero fucks what I think."

Emmet sighed while holding his eyes shut. "Then what harm can come from hearing the man out? You'd be doing me a favor."

"You're so smooth," I said, matching his sigh. "Don't think I don't see how you work it, Groshek. Really, though? All shifter Alphas are the worst. Everyone knows it. They're famous for their arrogance, their patriarchal world view and, frankly, their duplicity. And that's not even mentioning when they become pack leaders, they develop hair-trigger tempers that always lead to murderous shows of force."

He shook his head. "I wish I could argue with that stereotype, but it's not far off for most pack leaders, but that's not

Cyrus. He's a new breed. And, besides, I'll be there, by your side, the whole time. I'll have your back."

Like the gallantry, but, dude, I got that covered.

"I'll literally have sex with you right now if I don't have to go."

Emmet's eyes widened. His brain went kaput.

"That was a joke," I clarified.

"Yeah, of course, I knew that." He gathered himself. "Listen, Cyrus didn't want me to tell you, but the pack has been hit with the dust. We have three comatose members. We deserve a place at that table, Sophie, and we have considerable resources to put at the Board's disposal. Not to mention primal hunting instincts."

"That *we* came out of your mouth pretty fast, Emmet."

"Stronger together, Sophie, isn't that always true? I have Cyrus convinced you're trustworthy. A pack doesn't trust non pack easily. If you reject him now, he might not offer his help again and we'd be weaker apart."

I hated it when he was right. "Stronger together? You sound like a spin doctor, not a medical doctor," I said. "Okay, you persistent pain in my ass, I'll do it, but I'm reserving the right to terminate at the slightest provocation."

Emmet flashed one of his most radiant smiles.

"Turn down that smile, you creepy lobbyist. Let the record show that I think this is a terrible idea and will lead to nothing."

Chapter 10

THE THUD STARTLED ME awake. I did not know if it had happened in a dream or in my apartment. Or, perhaps, it was a result of my exploding headache.

I staggered out of bed in a daze, barely feeling my extremities. A numbing chill overtook my body. My teeth chattered and my bones began to ache.

A stifling silence filled my ears. A folded note had been slipped under the door. Bending to pick it up made my head spin. I didn't bother to peek outside as I knew, beyond the shadow of a doubt, that whoever left the note would be long gone.

I walked back to my bed shivering, worrying I would shatter from the growing cold, and even fearing frostbites.

I wrapped a blanket around me, then plopped down on the couch.

The folded note now sat near my feet. I stared at the piece of paper, waiting for warmth to chase away the chill.

When my body stopped shaking, I sat up and snatched the note into my hands.

My heart pounded in my ears as I straightened out the paper. The note was etched in blood. Memories of the last time I had received a blood note flooded my brain. I held my breath as I read.

To awaken the Diviner
The Lord of the Soul Swallowers
Must get his due
32°37'56.8"N
116°54'01.2"W

Coordinates. An exchange. My life for Faion's. The Lord of the Soul Swallowers knew who and what I was. Any last illusions of staying anonymous were gone forever. My life was forfeit.

The knock at the door felt expected. My body warmed quickly as I threw my blanket aside. I tried to quiet my heartbeat down. I walked through my apartment with a wave of energy already rushing to my fingertips.

I am ready. I am destruction.

Penelope Osvaldo pushed past me as I opened the door.

"You can put your nails away, kitten," she said. "It is I."

She held an empty grocery bag and a bright green watering can.

"Miss Penelope," I said, relaxing my energy. "What on earth?"

She looked smaller than she seemed at her enchanted house. No, she *was* smaller, extremely underweight and older. That house invigorated her.

I need to get me an enchanted house.

She wore a patterned, sunflower dress and a wide-brimmed hat adorned with daisies and peonies. A springtime sparkle leapt from her to chase the last of my chill away.

Penelope walked my studio apartment like it was a boutique museum. She took her time, assessing the furniture and valuing the sentiments in the art prints on the wall. She admired the Japanese Shoji screen that shielded my bedroom from my living area.

"Am I still dreaming?" I said, pushing my hair back. "Are you here?"

Penelope sat on the couch. "Where else would I be?"

I tried to clear my head. "Okay, yeah. And to what circumstance do I owe the pleasure?"

She frowned. "I am here to warn you, *mi hija*, but my aversion to protracted phone conversations is as steady as a deep river current."

A sign on my forehead must read: Please, warn me.

Penelope sniffed something in the air. She removed her hat, then withdrew a silver pin from her neatly braided hair.

She pricked her middle finger with the pin. The drop

of blood that spouted from her finger crackled as it turned to a coral vapor, expanding as it went airborne, and colored the light of dawn streaming through the half-drawn blinds a creamy rose.

A supernatural force hit me in the gut. I clutched my chest.

"You can feel it," Penelope said through clenched teeth. "My blood opposes a sinister force lingering in your abode, a necromantic spell as old as the first mages."

My lungs failed to draw breath, burning as if full of volcanic ash.

Penelope returned the pin to her hair. Her face betrayed a quiet serenity as if nothing meaningful was happening. "Fear not, witchling. The wicked blood that carried the spell to your home is already dissolving in the ether. The foul trick was not of today or yesterday. It is days old and it is fizzling out. *Una muerte rápida*. It no longer compromises your core energy."

The blood note... some poor soul had been sacrificed for this, and how many more would follow? I wanted to scream my scorched lungs out.

Penelope's hands quickly flourished in front of her face. The morning light returned to normal and the crushing force abated.

I could breathe again, and my headache vanished.

"There," she said, "the spell retreats, back in time, to ancient catacombs."

My grateful eyes landed on hers. "Thank you."

"*De nada, viajera ingenua.*"

I stared at her.

Penelope interlocked her fingers in her lap. "You want to know my warning, I think."

I nodded.

"*Bueno*, the vision came to me in my garden in the form of a one-eyed raven. Strange, yes? But for me, this happens. The wingspan of the bird was wider than the roof of the house. He fluttered his enormous wings over my head until they blocked out the sun. The one eye burned with a fire to make Hephaestus blush. It overtook my mind and forced me to bear witness as black demon hounds slaughtered a gazelle herd. Such grotesque carnage. Then the raven barked hoarsely, his jaw opened wide and I saw his bloodied fangs. I could even smell them. It was then I knew the bird was a black demon messenger and his Lord was not far."

The seer began to tremble. She inhaled quickly and re-peatedly. "The Shadow Lord, the scourge with dominion over demons and hounds alike watches you, Luna Mae, with a greater clairvoyance than I can understand."

"A supercharged pervert. Sounds about right."

"You mask terror with humor," she said. "You must hear me. I felt his presence in the garden as sure as I am feeling yours now."

Penelope won. I felt the terror. *Thanks for that.*

She had no idea that Chaos could watch me using his

third-eye vision to reach through vast distances to check on me. He stole that perilous power from Horror, the one being who could pull Chaos into his own obliteration if he made one false move.

"He senses you, *mi niña*, like a mother senses a child in her womb. You can hide nothing from him. He knows everything, even your fears."

If he sensed I was in danger, would he lift a finger to help? Or was I only a curiosity to him? Was he only watching to protect his investment?

I reached under the couch cushion and pulled out the blood note. "This was the bearer of the necromantic essence," I said and handed it to her.

The seer opened the note. Her only noticeable reaction to the words was a slight quiver of her lips.

Her open palm hovered over the creased paper. Her lips murmured:

"Devonia, amartia, eksatmos, anahorisia."

The blood-etched markings flickered, the scarlet color of the words faded into pink, then darkened to purple, as Penelope drew out the residual evil with her incantation and defused it.

"These coordinates they give to you," she said in a voice so low I barely heard her. "Do you know where this is?"

I shook my head. "No, but Google surely does."

"Basic maps won't take you there, senseless child. Only your mind will. It's the enchanted rotunda at Lower Otay

Lake. An unhewn pathway only supernatural eyes can find will lead you into the haunted round."

"Good thing I have some supernatural peepers then," I quipped.

She completely ignored me. "Only charmed folk wielding exceptional powers can enter without damaging their essence."

I'm kind of a big deal. I got this covered.

Penelope's eyes darkened, suddenly losing focus completely. She entered a mid-trance state. "Once inside the structure, there will be only you, none can help, none can reach you. You will be lost in a labyrinth. All reverberations in the rotunda are sealed. Your wits will be your power. The exit is cloaked by invisible wards. For centuries, it was an Immortal reformatory until the Great Eternal Magistrate shut it down in favor of the exile vortex. All who enter the rotunda must find their own way out. You need a pure spirit. It is a world removed and unconnected from all other worlds. *Only in truth.* Hold those words steadfast... for only a true heart can ever escape the round."

I had to swallow and lick my dry lips just to speak. "Sounds like I've found the perfect spring break getaway."

Seriously, the warped time vortex was child's play next to this place.

Penelope exited her trance-like state and glared at me. "It's a trap."

Ya think? "I know that. It's like literary a trap. Not

metaphorically. It was designed and built to be a trap, but I have no choice. It's my life for Celia's grandson."

Penelope nodded. "The diviner, yes, I think so. Do not make haste. Talk to your Shadow Warrior. He knows much and can guide you."

Not Winter. Not this time. I've turned to him too much.

"He's gone, and I wouldn't know where to start looking."

"Listen, child, I have no dominion over Immortal structures. Find a way to get to him, *brujita*. Only he might have insight into this labor."

And how would I do that? Unless I followed him to the equinoctial observatory—wherever the hell that was. I'd most likely just get lost on the way or end up putting us both in lethal jeopardy.

None of that was necessary. I had a spare Shadow Warrior lurking in the ether of my messed-up life. One that was always desperate to get on my good side. The only possible problem with my plan was that I had no way of sensing his whereabouts or even sending a message that would reach him.

Penelope said he lingered nearby in the spirit of the one-eyed bird in her garden or some other sort of wackiness. Uber had no chance to deliver me to that destination. And what exactly did *nearby* refer to when spoken by a seer in regard to an Immortal?

San Diego? Central America? Canada? Kathmandu? Planet Earth?

"I'll do my best," I finally said.

Penelope stood up, gathered her things and walked to the door.

"And when your best is not enough? What then?"

I was fresh out of answers.

"*Mi padre*, he drank too much and had a reputation of a fool, but years before, he had been in the war, he had been a hero. One day, he looked into my eyes and he made me listen. He told me these words. *The brave die faster*."

And just like that, the seer walked out the door.

Chapter 11

Neutral territory, that's what Emmet had promised when I agreed to meet with the head of the local pack. I hardly thought the abandoned ruins of a former pack HQ near the Mexican border qualified as neutral.

"Was there an apocalypse here or just your last meeting?" I asked.

"This happened before we were even born," he said. "There was a rift between the Tijuana and San Diego packs that escalated back in 1990. Properties were damaged, lives were lost. After a few hostile months, the packs came to an agreement."

The four-story building was partially collapsed as if it had been pounded by a wrecking ball. Rubble was piled and scattered everywhere. The stench of sewage hung in the air.

"This way," Emmet said as he walked through a rusty gate into a yard overgrown with weeds and wildflowers. From there, we stepped over and weaved around bent metal and broken cinder blocks to reach a back entrance to the empty building.

Inside there was a cleared space among twisted metal debris that had been pushed aside. Sunlight creeped through holes and cracks in the walls. There were no signs that there had ever been windows in this place.

I walked to a map that had been taped to a wall. There were post-it notes stuck to the edges of the map with directions to places I'd never heard of and a list of "people to contact". All the names were strange like Mambat or Zenar. The map itself was of a city I didn't recognize.

Emmet checked his phone. "Cyrus is running late."

Fucking shifters, trying to assert dominance.

"Who holds a meeting in a deathly place like this?"

"Cyrus chose the venue. He said no one comes here anymore."

"And yet we do," I said under my breath. "Hey, what's this guy's animal form?" I was more bored than curious.

Emmet grinned. "Oh, I would never spoil that."

Huh? Did King Shifty intend to show up full beasty boy to throw me off and intimidate me? What was this, amateur hour?

"This was such a bad idea," I said.

"No, trust me on this. You'll dig it," Emmet said, the grin on his face getting more obnoxious by the second.

Zero chance I dig it. I'd never seen him so easily pleased. Was he already under the spell of pack instincts? Would he turn as wild and attacking as the rest of them when they arrived?

I avoided walking through a tangled mess of spider webs, finding a way around them to get to the back of the room. "How big is the local pack?"

Emmet followed close behind me. I got a whiff of Irish Spring soap and a subtle and spicy scent of cologne. *Focus, Sophie, focus.* He had a gentle masculinity and unintended charm that could be irresistible.

"Five-hundred strong," he said.

"Damn," I said. "That's not a pack, it's a brigade."

"The biggest pack in the state," he added. "Maybe even in the country."

And Cyrus was their exalted leader. Wonderful. Hierarchy was a form of religion for shapeshifters. If he ordered them to hold their pee, they'd faithfully obey until their bladders burst.

Shapeshifting packs could be formidable opponents. They acted as one and had unmatched hunting instincts. You didn't want them hunting you. I'd have to limit my sarcasm in order not to set Cyrus off.

A deep howl bellowed outside. Was he a wolf? A coyote? A hyena, maybe?

"Shit traffic on the freeway," a deep, male voice said behind me.

I spun around as he stepped into view with long, relaxed strides. He was in his human form and younger than I expected, early thirties maybe, with a surprisingly non-threatening face. Of course, appearances were not to be trusted with shapeshifters. They could rip your throat out the moment you let your guard down.

Cyrus was tall and fit—no surprise there. You didn't get to be the leader of a large shifter pack without being an exceptional specimen.

I checked him out, making no attempt to hide my suspicion. He had wavy, light brown hair, dark eyes, black jeans, a black leather biker jacket, and two slightly crooked front teeth that, somehow, when combined with his uneven facial features, made him look handsome.

"My morning was a beast," he said with a slight grin.

"Been there," I said.

He walked around me. "You are Sophie."

"Last time I checked," I said.

He lost interest and walked to the map.

Was he worried I might contaminate him with my insignificance?

"You are Cyrus," I said, mocking his patronizing tone.

He studied the map. "Are you a wise one, Sophie?"

"Depends which professor you ask."

He turned around. I approached him with an extended arm, offering a handshake. We needed to reboot this shaky introduction pronto.

Cyrus recoiled as if my arm were a venomous snake.

"No offense, but I prefer not to make physical contact

with a witch. It's an unnecessary risk."

How very medieval of him.

"Sounds like we should make this short," I said, fighting my temper.

He circled me, slowly, like a predator cat. "Emmet thinks a lot of you. He tells me I should trust you."

"Trust this, Cyrus," I said. "Walk around me again and it will most definitely be an unnecessary risk for you."

"Oh, there it is," he said, pleased. "The fire you were trying to hide."

Another alpha, playing man games. I'm so over it.

"Emmet," I said. "I'm ready to go."

"Cyrus," Emmet said. "It wasn't easy getting her here."

"I should think not," Cyrus said. "Her heartbeat hasn't increased. This is not her first spitting match."

"I liked it better when you were howling," I said, losing interest.

Three other shifters stepped out of the shadows and closed in instinctively. Cyrus held out his hand to make them stand down. "Unless I saw your teeth, I could never believe you had the leverage with magic leadership Emmet suggested."

"Emmet sees what he wants to see. I'm a low-level witch who lives in the basic world. Not exactly a Deep Down influencer."

"Maybe so, but you're no average co-ed," he said, deep in thought. "Your interactions with the Immortal councils would clearly fall outside your college curriculum. The undying have a greater interest in you, but rest assured you will be primed for elimination once they have tired of you."

"Immortal councils? You're definitely barking up the wrong tree."

I immediately regretted that.

"Perhaps you would prefer my bite," he said, unamused.

"A threat? You might be slow to react in such constricting leather."

No matter how flattering it was on a strapping man like Cyrus, leather would probably slow any wild expansion of muscle and bone.

Now I saw *his* fire glimmering in his eyes. "In less than one second I can be au naturel."

"I'd only need half a second to skewer you whole."

The side of his mouth lifted, revealing a sharp tooth. "You are fortunate my restraint is uncommon for a Higher Alpha."

Emmet stepped between us. "Can we all chill a little? Let's remember why we're here. This is a good faith meeting."

"Easy," Cyrus told Emmet. "Or I might think you're commanding me."

Oh, the arrogant prick.

Emmet held the Alpha's stare. I was proud and a little impressed.

Easy, girl. Not why you're here.

"I promised Sophie she'd be respected," Emmet said forcefully.

"She has my respect," Cyrus said. "Now I need everyone to go outside and give us some privacy. That includes you, Emmet."

I gave Emmet a little smile and a nod to reassure him. The last thing I wanted was to create friction between him and his Higher Alpha.

The moment we were alone, Cyrus took a running start, jumped up, bounded off a wall and landed right in front of me. His eyes flashed a deep red, then flared back to brown. It happened so fast I forgot to react.

"Emmet's a good man but a terrible judge of character," he said.

I nodded. "Apparently. He said you were cool, for instance."

He wasn't amused. "Control your urges. Stay away from him."

The fuck? I'm this close to neutering this pup.
"You're a dick."

"I'm not the one putting him at risk."

Tears threatened to well in my eyes. I hated that he was right.

"What is this?" I said. "Another threat?"

Cyrus cracked his knuckles. "Threats are for the desperate and weak. I'm about real talk."

"Dude, your bedside manner is atrocious. Wasn't the

point of this whole stupid meeting so you can ask me for help?"

He laughed. *Really, Cyrus, now you laugh?*

"Your help? You need our help. Shifters tend to dominate the natural sciences. I can put our best people on it right away. We have shifters at university research centers, government labs and NASA."

Holy shit, I knew shifters had friends in high places, but I never knew they had it like that. *Even NASA? Okay.*

"Alright, Cyrus, let's get to it, then. What did you have in mind?"

He crossed his arms on his chest. "I don't like the way you say *Cyrus*. There's a quality in your voice, a lack of respect."

You noticed?

"Fine, Mr. McDonnell, Sir, what did you have in mind?"

He closed his eyes and exhaled. "I have five hundred and eighteen shifters under my command and protection. More than half inside the compound, the rest situated within the borders of San Diego County."

"Your little fiefdom."

He grinded his teeth. "My territory, yes. I provide organization and protection. I keep them safe. We have no allies. We live in this world only, not in some sad, subterranean exile. We have nowhere to hide. The pack depends on me. And now I have three in a coma and the rest anxious and paranoid. They feel like sitting ducks. So, forgive me if I am not as cool as usual when meeting a friend of a packmate.

This enemy is neither visible nor physical, and we're all in the dark. My trust has run thin."

Finally, the real talk he promised.

"I get it. I do. None of us are enjoying these attacks."

"We need to be a part of those meetings in the Deep Down. My gut screams that the pack is vital to the success of any plan being hatched to defeat the dust. In exchange, we will use our instincts to hunt for an antidote in the lab and I myself will help you hunt the invisible assailants."

I pressed my fingers against my forehead. "Sure, sounds great. I'll do my best, Cyrus, I really will, but you must understand that I am twenty-three and have little sway in the under realm or anywhere else. I think I, or at least someone close to me, can present your case to the Board of Supernatural Orders, but that's where my value ends."

"Very well," he said, a little disappointed. "That will have to do."

Before I could respond, he turned his back on me and began shedding his clothing while he strode away. First the jacket, then the jeans, then the t-shirt went flying. It took him more like three seconds to strip down than the one he had promised. Men and their promises.

I got a delightful eyeful of his firm gluteus maximus and muscled back and broad shoulders. His body twitched and his tan skin stretched as black fur spurted out, covering him from head to toe. It took my breath away.

Claws slid out and snapped in place. The huge predatory

feline pounced for the exit in a single leap and vanished in the blink of an eye.

No wonder Emmet thought I'd be entertained. I mean, c'mon! Cyrus McDonnell was a ghost of the forest and a legend of pop culture—a majestic, fierce black panther.

I WIPED DOWN MY sword with a rag lightly saturated in gun oil. The slow, repetitive motion of the cloth rubbing the blade dulled my senses. My mouth tasted like the lavender scented candles burning on my coffee table.

It was dead quiet outside. The only thing audible was the humming of the wards I had bound to the walls, door and windows of my apartment. If anyone tried to sneak in, they'd be the star of my barbecue.

The phone rang a second time after I had ignored the first.

"Yep?" I said after clicking on the call.

"I get a yep?" Lily said. *"Did I bang your boyfriend or something?"*

I set the sword in my lap and rested my hand on the handle. "I don't have one of those," I said. "You're good."

Lily hesitated. *"Is everything okay with Faion?"*

The faster I pulled the Band-Aid off the better. "Yeah, false alarm."

"He had me worried. Where is he now?"

"Um, Easter. He went with Celia some place for Easter."

"*Some place?*" she said, unsure. "*You mean Oregon.*"

"Yeah," I said. "Didn't I say that?"

"*Are you going to Oregon, too?*"

Why was there suspicion in Lily's voice?

"Ah, yeah. I'm going, too."

My hesitation to answer cost me. She saw right through me.

"*Sophie, you suck at keeping secrets. What's up?*"

I so hated having to dismiss her concern with another lie. "Headache."

"*Huh, a headache, and I'm not even trying to sleep with you,*" she said. Her voice held a gravity I had never heard before. "*We always play this game, Soph, but I've always known there's more to you than we talk about.*"

I tried to laugh. "Watching Dexter doesn't make me a serial killer."

Lily sighed. "*Nice try. It's okay, you'll talk to me when you're ready.*"

I held my eyes closed, wanting to confess every detail when I heard the three hang-up beeps. She was gone. Our friendship was skating on thin ice and I sucked at skating. The inevitability of losing everything overwhelmed me.

A sharp pain in my right hand made my eyes drop. My hand had slid from the handle to the blade. A ribbon of blood painted the sword crimson.

The cut in my palm healed quickly. Why couldn't I just keep bleeding like everyone else? Why couldn't I have friends and dreams and be anonymous like everyone else? I wanted scars—the big heartbreaks, the small victories. I wanted to find silver linings after failing. I wanted all the basic fears and all the wonders of the frail and the fleeting.

I wanted one mortal life, was that too much to ask?

Chapter 12

THE ENCHANTED ROTUNDA STOOD inside a stone circle. The secret path that led me there flared in and out of dimensional existence, winding through a ghost forest below the rocky bluffs near Lower Otay Lake. The forest itself was only visible to supernatural beings. Every time I put my foot down, shrubs and trees shifted apart to clear a path. A bioluminescent fungus glowed to life ahead of me to guide my way.

The rotunda was a tall, round building made of brown mudbricks with a clay tile roof shaped like a bowl. At first glance, it looked too small for it to be anything other than a grain bin or a sweat lodge. It surely didn't have the space to house an elaborate maze or an army of soul swallowers.

A vibrant green moss and snaking vines crawled on the walls, shimmering with magic. Tiny ice flies hovered around the burnt orange doorframe.

Cobblestone paths circled the rotunda and led to flower

gardens in the back where birds sang peacefully. The whole scene gave the impression of an idyllic pastoral landscape that veiled dark secrets.

A breeze rustled the leaves on the path ahead of me. A voice, a baritone chant, broke through the quiet. I raised my palm to direct a splash of energy at the building. The door opened slowly accompanied by a prolonged creaking.

I filled my lungs with oxygen and my magic core with as much elemental energy as possible. The overload of power made me feel giddy. The rotunda fostered the same undiluted magic as Serenity Valley, not in the same concentrated abundance but enough to get a witch drunk on the elements.

The open door invited me into a world of sinister secrets. I stepped cautiously, then took one long stride into the forbidden chamber.

The door closed and disappeared with an echoing screech. The space I stood in was empty, dimly lit by an unknown source. The walls were covered with flowery wallpaper which completely disorientated me.

How is this the same building I saw from the outside?

Dust rose as the room began to spin. I stumbled to keep my feet until it stopped and a new door opened.

A shockwave thrust me forward. I clutched the doorframe with both hands to hang on. I fought to hold my grip until I remembered Faion. I decided to let go. I had come this far. There was no turning back now.

I tumbled into a new room which was a cozy suburban

living room with an azure marine life wallpaper and a crackling fireplace.

Slowly, the spinning began again. The place was like a giant centrifuge. My feet left the ground as I whirled, and when I landed, I was sitting in a long metal corridor. Everything was silver. Reflected light flooded my vision as I tried to climb back to my feet.

The corridor began to stretch, causing the walls to crack open. The jagged gaps grew large enough for me to walk through—not that I'd do that willingly.

Aggressive magic licked at my skin. The sensation stung and sent shivers down my spine. I tested my own magic and found it ready and willing as it drank in more energy from the abundant stream of magic in the rotunda.

The gaps began to fill with surging white light. Mirror doors appeared as the gaps fused together. Other mirror doors of all sizes began to emerge from the walls up and down the corridor.

My reflection appeared everywhere in an endless, flickering loop that made my eyes ache until I closed and covered them. When I looked again, a double wrought iron gate loomed in front of me.

I could hear the wards guarding the gate in crisscrossing patterns. There were too many to count. I could try to break them, but I'd be revealing my etheric essence to them, like I did fighting the wards at the Sacred Vault. There was no way I was going to reveal my true heritage to the soul swallowers.

Cursing under my breath, I started cataloguing the wards in my head one by one, preparing myself for hours of work. Without warning, all the wards dissipated, *poof*, and the gate swung open.

Determined to find my way, I stepped through the gate. I stopped cold in my tracks. I had stepped out of and back into the very same corridor.

Such bullshit.

By now my patience was running thin. I yanked one of the mirror doors open and walked through it, only to end up at the exact same spot. I tried door after door, always with the same result.

I took a deep breath to block it all out. The Lord of the soul swallowers had buried me in an illusion of smoke and mirrors. What forgotten magic did I possess that could possibly free me?

Even closing my eyes didn't stop the world from spinning. I felt dizzy and off balance until an idea came to me—the ley lines. Finesse was never my lane. Go big or stay home... *am I right?* If I could latch onto a ley line point, my turbo-charged magic would blow these riddles sky high.

I could shut down the rotunda for good.

I sent my core sensors as far as they would travel, letting my energy run wild as I searched for a signal from the nearest ley line. Nothing. I concentrated harder. My jaw stiffened and my ears started to ache as I gave it all I had. About to give up and collapse, I found and anchored onto a ley line.

The rotunda reacted angrily as my energy surged. A cataclysmic outpouring of screams filled the space. I cupped my ears with my hands to keep my eardrums from busting. Everything spun one more time. When I regained my balance, I was standing outside—but where?

The sun burned down scorching hot. My boots trod on fine golden sand. A line of dry bluffs loomed ahead. A smoky cloud flared where the horizon met the hilltops.

This was precisely what Penelope had warned. My tricks were of no use here. There was no help coming, no way out except the one I might find in my heart, whatever that meant. In retrospect, heeding her words and waiting for Winter's return before embarking on this folly made a lot of sense.

Something stirred beneath my feet. I jumped aside. The creature expanded like a giant snake slithering inside the sand. Magic streamed from my hands, searing the trail of the unseen threat.

The sand split open. A geyser of steam shot upwards. A quiet melody reached my ears as from within the earth. Something choked me. The melody, the steam and the sand all worked together to hypnotize. The spell clutched onto me, bonding my feet to the ground. My willpower faltered and my whole body yearned to be pulled into the earth and laid to rest.

The figure of a man in the distance flickered in and out of existence. He strode towards me from the far-off bluffs. His gait was languid but assured.

I tried to get my bearings. I scanned the landscape for anything familiar. Nothing. Just me and him on the scorching sand.

My feet were stuck. All I could do was ball up my hands, then hold them out as I loaded my tingling fists with an electric current.

The man came to a halt five feet away. He was average in every facet. Average height, average weight and balding. He wore a long white tunic that hung on him like it was two sizes too big. His face was a blank canvas, unwrinkled and impassive. I was sure he had no wrinkles because not a single feeling had ever registered on that face. His eyes were small, his chin weak and his nose thin and aquiline.

The man bowed and grinned, revealing cracked lips and decayed teeth.

"The Almighty Lord of the Soul Swallowers welcomes the witch who is no witch to his Boundless Kingdom," he said with a parched voice. "We truly hope you'll find your new home less than comfortable."

"I guess no point in asking about air conditioning," I said.

His cackling had an echo to it, like he had two throats. "A sharp tongue will lead to many hearty beatings. We will enjoy you, pitiful witch. You'll make a good pet."

I licked my lips. "Now I am curious... Is the Almighty Lord of Lameness as ugly and wretched of a motherfucker as you are? Because that would explain why he's so pissed off at everything and everyone."

The cackling stopped. "Insolence will be answered with pain."

I'm so tired of all this shit.

My energy rushed to my feet, freeing them. "You have a one-track mind," I said, then pounced on him, wielding a high voltage lightning bolt in my right hand.

Before he knew what was happening, I pressed the sizzling bolt against his throat.

"Take me to your sadistic boss if you want to keep your head," I said.

The man crowed uncontrollably. He put both his hands on the bolt and ran it clean through his own neck.

I watched, mortified, as his head fell off and rolled onto the sand. The rest of his body stood upright for what seemed like five seconds, before toppling to the ground and shriveling down to a rat-sized carcass. The tunic caught fire and burned to vapor within seconds.

Two men identical to the first in every detail strode towards me. The bastards were like the Hydra—you cut off one head and two emerge to take its place.

"There's no escape, witch," they said with the same voice as the first.

More and more emerged, surrounding me, speaking the same words with the same voices out of the same faces.

Curse my stubborn arrogance!

Why did I ever come to this hellish place on my own? Penelope's words rang in my ears. *It's a trap, Luna! A trap!*

I needed to at least stall them. I saw an opening and I took it, bolting for the bluffs. I wouldn't use my mist magic unless I ran out of options.

I made it to the foothills of the central bluff where I used a sand mound as a barricade. I created a thick shield around me and waited. My knees trembled as I struggled to breathe steadily.

The uglies took their time. They dragged their feet as if they just woke to take the garbage out. In their eyes I posed no threat.

They came to a halt only feet away from the bluff. They raised their hands above their heads, letting out a collective wailing howl. My blood froze. The howl hung in the air as dark clouds gathered, hiding the sun.

Other voices screamed from atop the bluffs. A different breed of soul swallowers loped down the slopes. These uglies were taller, bulkier and they carried long-bladed spears and heavy axes.

I cringed as their war cries drew closer. If they all came at once, how long could I survive without exposing my true essence?

They all stopped as one. A single ugly stepped out in front of the others to spread out his arms and begin chanting. A sudden reflex had me hurl a single energy pulse that struck his right arm and knocked him to the ground.

Another soul swallower stepped forward and another and another. I kept hurling energy, but every time one went down, two more took their place.

Any act of resistance on my part increased the odds against me. Every victory was defeat. I lost track of time. The hideous soul swallowers kept multiplying. There would be thousands within minutes.

Least enchanting rotunda ever!

I channeled every available resource within and assaulted the foul bastards with hefty waves of energy. My blasts expanded wider and wider, striking the advancing battalion from every possible angle.

Thunder ripped across the sky followed by a whirlwind that plunged down to swallow up all my energy blasts in midair before promptly sending them straight back at me.

My own magic tore into my shield with magnified force, nearly splitting it open with a power that would have blown me to pieces.

"Surrender, skinny witch, and save the diviner," a soul swallower hissed. "You came here for this, don't fight it."

You don't know me, fugly. I've got my own plans.

"The Lord will not be pleased," another one croaked.

I blew up his mouth with a fireball, setting his face on fire.

"Eat a bag of dicks, fucking ass-kisser!"

Didn't realize I had that in me.

His shrieks curdled my blood as he shrank to a burnt carcass. Something changed. No replacements arrived. Was it only death by fire that would stop the endless regenerations?

Of course, the one magic I hated.

A horde of giant grasshoppers the size of my fist burst from behind the ranks of the soul swallowers. They raced up the bluff, swarming me. I sliced at them from within my weakened shield with thin strings of laser energy, splitting body after body in half.

Sweat ran down my lip and forehead as I blasted the critters off. I realized too late they were only a distraction for some jacked-up, stouter soul swallowers that had encircled me. I leapt off the slope, tumbling down rocky terrain that gouged my arms and legs, injured my back and stung my tail bone.

The pain was real. I was running out of options. They chased after me. I ran with a severe limp, turning back when I could to let loose pulsating green energy that knocked a few off their feet.

It was too little, too late. Their numbers were too great, and my healing was too slow in my depleted state.

Nothing here ever fucking dies! Everything multiplies!

They would stall me, wear me out, and eventually extract every last secret hidden inside me, all the way down to my true essence. I was getting a hard lesson in why they were called soul swallowers.

No one was coming to the rescue. I created this hot fucking mess and I alone would have to clean it up. I remembered an old training. Tam would be proud. I built an active blue energy field tight around me that reacted to anything that moved toward me.

Every time the uglies grabbed at me, their grimy hands got blasted. It worked. I decided to run right through them when a stabbing blast of dark magic suddenly pulverized my shield. I had to use last-second hand energy to deflect it away from my energy core.

That was it. I was surrounded by dense mobs of vicious fiends obeying a master necromancer who, I was sure, would show up at any moment to fight me in my feeble state. I gave up even thinking about escape. My spirit was not pure, and my heart was not true or whatever it needed to be.

All I had left was pain and hate—at myself mostly.

My tired eyes fell on a soul swallower engulfed in a purple shield. His face was unique, not like the others. He uncorked a bottle with his teeth and dipped the tip of his spear in it. When he pulled the blade out, it shone silver with sparkling specks of toxic dust.

A shadow swept across the mob. Someone landed right next to me.

"Friends of yours?" *That voice.* It could only be one man.

The soul swallower raised the silver-tipped spear, poised to strike. His eyes fixed suddenly on the glistening Damascus sword just before it cracked open his skull. The mythic sword slashed and gashed again and again as Chaos whirled and pounced, chopping off heads like he was collecting ripe fruit.

He whizzed around like a demon, impish grin on his face, the tails of his black trench coat flapping about him, his black boots sinking into sand wet with the gooey insides of the slaughtered soul swallowers.

No, not a demon—Chaos looked like a primitive god, an immortal warrior king on a bloody path of revenge.

A soul swallower managed to graze the tip of his spear against Chaos's cheek before sinking it into the Shadow Warrior's neck. Crimson ribbons swelled on Chaos's face and neck, spreading down his chest and arms.

"Nice foreplay," Chaos said, grinning at the spearman. "My turn."

He pressed his big hand on the gushing gash on his neck, then vanished inside a puff of blue smoke.

A heartbeat later, he materialized behind the soul swallower and hacked off every appendage, starting with each arm, then each leg. The spearman fell to the ground nothing more than a stump with a head, still alive, a stunned expression lingering on his face even after Chaos chopped off his head.

Ten feet away, a man fell from the sky and landed on his feet.

Chaos scooped me up with one arm. "Hold on, daft witch."

I wrapped my arms around his bloodied neck. My exhausted head fell against his chest. My heavy eyelids fell, too, just as the world started spinning inside a cool blue mist.

Chapter 13

WHEN MY EYES OPENED, the smoke had cleared, and Chaos set me down on the roof of a luxury hotel complete with an infinity pool and a tropical-island-style cocktail bar.

"What? How?" I said.

Chaos flashed me a toothy grin. "I have tricks for days, moon kitten."

I looked past him and saw the Pacific Ocean stretching out in all its afternoon glory. Behind me a seaside road was busy with traffic. I walked to the edge of the roof and guessed the luxury hotel had about four floors.

Everything hurt. Blood stained my tattered jeans, jacket, shirt and shoes. My hands were caked in blood. Beneath the blood were aches and sharp pains and sweat, lots of sweat, sweat everywhere. My wet hair clung to my forehead, ears and neck.

Chaos was even filthier. From his long dark hair down to his black leather boots he was plastered in reeking soul swallower entrails and putrid blood.

I suddenly remembered Faion. I pushed Chaos, then pounded hard on his chest. "Take me back! You maniac! Take me back! I'm serious, Chaos. Right now! I need to be there. I had a plan! Damn you!"

Chaos stepped back. "Oy, relax, girl. Unless your plan was to be a pinata, it was not working out. You're welcome, by the way."

"I was losing on purpose, you bozo!"

He creased his forehead. "Then you were wildly success-ful."

Why do I even try?

"You're an Immortal pain. I was waiting for the Lord of the Soul Swallowers to show his face and I'm pretty sure that he was finally there and that's when you scooped me up without my consent."

He tapped my forehead. "I think I hear an echo," he said. "You had nary an idea who it was you were fighting."

"Oh, really? Well, why don't you enlighten me?"

"That flying freakshow back there that you call Lord of wiggly-wop or whatnot was Cerber."

"So, yet another ancient prick known by many names."

"So... he would have had your empty little head on a spike, before boxing it up and having it sent to Papa Winter. He would cube the rest of your body to scatter inside the lair of the three-headed hounds of Hades—but not before he drew out your essence bit by bit, nerve-by-nerve until he could use it to cloak himself and sneak through the portals to your under realm where he would put on his barbeque bib and start munching on every crunchy little dancing faerie and prancing troll that crossed his path."

Okay, well, I didn't know all that.

"Düsternis would get what he always wanted." I said. "Absolute dominion over Immortals and mortals alike."

My words amused him. "Wrong yet again. The only useful thing that dodgy twit Cerber ever did was to throw a wrench into Düsternis' plan to expand his authority. The odium between the two is quite nasty."

Winter had said the same thing. The light dawned on me. "So Cerber is not only the Lord of the Soul Swallowers, he's also one of the three Chief Necromancers who were once granted access to the Eternal Halls."

There was pride in his eyes. "Look who's just arrived."

I held my index finger half an inch apart from my thumb. "I was this close," I said. "This close to getting him, Chaos."

"What nonsense is this? Wait, yes, I see it now. Winter, that true believer, he's done this to you. He's inflated your ego to the point of self-destruction?" He grabbed my shoulders. "Stay away from Cerber. Understand? His power comes at you with a complexity you can't fathom. You are in no way ready. Even if you had a mist horse and some training, you would be wise to ride that horse the other way. Stay clear, Luna. And stop letting that delusional old friend of ours skew your judgment."

I swiped his hands off me. "You were there. We could have done the job together. You were supposed to be my secret weapon."

He seemed genuinely perplexed. "That was your plan?"

"You came, didn't you? You and your shadow magic and third-eye vision and all that badass shit only you can do. I've seen you wield dark magic and fight off necromancy. The soul swallowers didn't fucking multiply when *you* killed them. Carnage is your thing, right? That's all you had to do."

"You spoiled millennials just order up everything on your little apps and expect it delivered lickety-split. Hope this doesn't ruin my rating."

I fought a smile, secretly relieved to have escaped that nightmarish rotunda.

"Besides," he continued, "I was in my spot, perfectly in the shade of a palm tree in Bora Bora when you hatched this lunacy that you call a plan."

"Sorry to interrupt time with one of your little playthings," I said.

"Three, I'll have you know. And Tahitian women are quite exquisite."

"Gross," I said under my breath. "You're like a perpetual teenager."

"A teenager should have it so good," he said. "The point is maybe you need to communicate better with the participants of your plans. Also, stop making plans. You're dreadful at it."

He stood at the very edge of the roof, facing the sea. "Just tell yourself it's all going to work out and enjoy life. That's what I do. It's time to drink in the sweet nectar of immortality. Every moment is infinite." He opened his arms to receive the soothing embrace of the gusting sea air.

I stood next to him to stare out at an incoming wave. It grew big, then curled and crashed before sliding quickly up the slope of the beach below.

"One of Cerber's victims is a dear friend," I said. "I wonder, have you ever had one of those?"

He stared at the sea and did not answer.

"I received a blood note. It promised I could exchange my life for my friend's life. Cerber is the same bastard who abducted Emmet, definitely in league with Horror, and now he's seen us together."

"Most unfortunate," he said, quietly. "What did they teach you at your Deep Down school? None should ever assume a necromancer will honor his word. For them, dishonesty is the virtue."

"Maybe I was a little impetuous," I admitted, "but I did hold back until you got there. I never let them see my true essence."

"That's good, but I already knew that," he said. "If Cerber had known your secret, he would have been there long before I showed up."

"I knew what I was doing. I told you."

He closed his eyes and shook his head.

"Okay, maybe I fucked up, but I know things," I said. "I know about your past with Horror and how you stole his gift of the third-eye vision. That's how I knew I could get you to show up."

Chaos growled, then spun around, grabbed a wicker umbrella from the bar and broke it over his knee. He threw both pieces over the bar, smashing a row of expensive liquor bottles.

I'd forgotten how volatile and dangerous he could be, and how he seemed to have an innate ability to throw me off balance.

He started pacing and talking to himself. "The infant witch says she put herself in danger *on purpose* to force me to her side. She throws the name of the Eternal menace around like it's girlish gossip. She presumes to know things. She thinks I can be manipulated."

"Ah, dude..."

Lightning quick, he wrapped his fingers around my throat and leaned me back over the edge of the building. My heels were barely still on the roof.

I grabbed onto his forearm to keep from falling.

He bared his teeth at me. "Why would you ever think I'd risk using such consuming power for your cat and mouse games?"

My voice came out strained. "Because you did it before. A seer sensed someone had been entering my mind. I knew it could only be you."

He released me and I began to fall. His other hand casually twisted open to produce a yellow energy lasso which darted out to wrap me around my waist and pull me back onto the roof.

"That's not how it works," he said.

I rubbed my neck. When I swallowed, it hurt. I decided enough was enough and just blurted it out. "Are you my father?"

Chaos stared at me, disgusted. Mirth suddenly broke out on his face. "Have you gone mad, cupcake? Your fucking father? Am I talking to a Star Wars fangirl?" He pulled on my ear. "I have fathered no offspring, and for that I am grateful. And no child of mine would ever be so painfully naïve."

"The seer saw it. You and I, we're related."

He brushed a hair off my face. "You overpaid for your seer."

"And yet your blood saved me," I said, uncertain.

"My blood is hyper regenerative. It healed you, nothing more. I don't go around lending it out, but for now I'm stuck with you. We're all trapped by our fates, mist rider."

Chaos walked straight off the edge of the roof and floated down to land his foot on the first narrow step of the fire escape.

He winked up at me before hurrying down the steps. I jumped down to the fire escape and chased after him. "How are we related?" I yelled.

He was already on the ground. "We're not."

"Why are you lying to me?"

He came to a halt and disappeared.

I stopped. "Damn."

He materialized right in front of me on the second-floor fire escape.

Chaos was taller than me even standing one step lower. "Do you want to be related, injured dove? Do you want to experience family bonding and use it as an excuse to dump your lousy mentor and come over to the dark side? Is that what this is about, Princess Leia?"

"I'm not a Star Wars fangirl, by the way. You can stop with all these word games. Just stop, please. First a diviner saw it and then a seer. We share the same blood. Frankly, I trust them more than I trust you."

He leapt off the fire escape and landed in a soft crouch two floors below.

I did the same without thinking. I landed hard and rolled onto my side. Things made cracking sounds.

"That hurt," I said, climbing to my feet.

"Use a touch of magic next time," he said.

"Good note." I took in a deep breath. "I'm starting to see it. You gave me to Winter, fully intending to come back for me one day. Let him do the heavy lifting developing my talents before Horror came back. I get it, but your nemesis came back too soon, didn't he? And I'm not ready and now you're afraid. The great Chaos is as full of fears as the rest of us. You thought you had time."

He yawned. "You're stuck on repeat."

"You're stuck on denial. You could have trained me. Why didn't you keep me if you knew how much you needed me?"

He walked out onto the sand. "I snatched you from your crib, Luna Mae. If I had not, you would have been killed or caged. All these words you've been spitting when a simple *thank you* would have sufficed. And now my new full-time job seems to be saving your ass again and again."

Finally, we're getting somewhere.

"Okay," I said. "Thank you and thank you and thank you. Who would have killed or caged me in my crib, Chaos? Who do you protect?"

He threw his hands in the air. "This is such tedium. We just established I protect *you*. Really, I've had better conversations with Siberian fur traders."

The blue smoke swirled, and Chaos vanished.

Run, but we're all trapped by our fates, Shadow Warrior.

Chapter 14

HELIANNA STACKED THE SCROLLS on the table in two piles. An extremely fit woman in her early forties and a pyromancer, Helianna was the Region's second-in-command. From her heavy eyelids and bloodshot eyes, it was obvious she hadn't had a proper night's sleep in days.

Besides the two of us, the only other people sitting around the unfinished wood conference table were Celia and two leaders of the Chronomaster Order, Grayson and Anya.

Grayson was in his thirties with sandy blond hair and astute eyes, and a time master of the higher order. Anya was a bit younger, dark skinned with a mane of dark hair framing gentle eyes and sensual lips.

Chronomasters had the innate ability to sense time's inner workings and could briefly halt it or alter its course, one of the most dangerous and devastating powers among magic creatures.

Helianna had just let us know that Horpheus wouldn't be

attending today's meeting. He was busy trying to decipher an ancient scroll that mentioned a similar substance to the silver dust.

I was included in the meeting on Celia's request that cited me as a witness to the aftermath of Faion's attack, but I bet there was more to it.

All magic users in the San Diego metro area had been notified of the threat of silver dust. Sentries had been placed in strategic spots. Powerful mages, sorcerers and witches who had rarely visited the basic world now roamed the streets, day and night.

Supernatural residents of San Diego had been instructed to stay inside and conjure wards for every door and window. The magic reverberations that would reach the Immortal councils or the Eternal halls were the least of the Board's concerns. It had been decades since such measures were taken.

Helianna considered all four of us one at a time. "As you well know, all of our scientific research units are working around the clock to neutralize the dust. In addition, our historians and academics are pouring through scrolls and footnotes with general mage healers by their side."

Anya nodded. "We are doing everything we can in the chronochambers, too."

"Yes," Helianna said. "Like everything else we are doing, it may amount to nothing, but there is something you can do together, all three of you, that may shed some light to assist all our researchers."

"All three of us?" Grayson said, glancing at me. "Tell us more."

"Luna Mae here is a very special young witch," Helianna said. "She was able to get within inches of the dust and yet shows no signs of contamination."

Alarms went off in my head. "Neither does Celia."

Helianna set a rolled-up scroll in front of her. "Not entirely equivalent, Luna. Celia wore a most rare protective amulet around her neck. Only the highest diviners possess such an amulet. And Celia is needed here for her rare gifts. You, however, had no such protection, yet remain unaffected. All other magic users who have come within ten feet of the dust have exhibited a variety of serious symptoms. Your good health tells us you have a natural immunity. On your way out we will take blood and tissue samples from you to be shared with appropriate teams to be studied."

Uh oh. Winter and Chaos would not like that.

I took a glance at Celia. She sat quietly, avoiding my eyes. Why had she told the Board everything after I had asked her to keep my name out of it?

It was true that I had a certain degree of immunity to the dust but not the kind that could be replicated. I couldn't tell the Board it was a mist rider thing.

I couldn't even tip them off about Horror and Cerber without betraying the fact I was their main target. Winter would have a fit if I spoke a single word on the subject, especially after going to the rotunda behind his back.

Grayson wiped his hand across the table. The hologram of an hourglass popped up. Grains of silver dust ran through its narrow neck.

"We tested the dust through the chronometer," he said. "We felt time ripples, which hatched the theory that the perpetrator is altering time to disperse the silver dust."

The many-aged man.

Anya swiped left. The hourglass hologram vanished, replaced by a glass vial filled with dust. "We believe we can aid in isolating the dust's molecular structure which our researchers could use to engineer an antidote."

I nodded. With them so far.

"Our problem," Grayson said, "is that we need an ample amount of silver dust and the researchers could only spare this small vial. We need more."

"How much more?" I said.

"The more the better," Anya said.

"Any amount we can get our hands on," Helianna added. "And the researchers need more, too."

The truth finally hit me. "Ah, you want me to help collect it."

Helianna bowed her head. "You are more than wanted. You are vital. Every time our kind gets near the dust, no matter the precautions taken, they get sick. The condition of some has worsened over time, leading to seizures and loss of hearing or vision. We know you live as a basic, but magic kind needs you."

Helianna had pitched me so hard I wanted her to believe her plea had convinced me, but the truth was I was all in all the time. "I can't know for sure I'm completely immune, but no matter, I will do as asked."

"I should have stated your cooperation is completely voluntary."

"Yes, ma'am. I assumed that to be the case."

Helianna sat back in her chair. "We're putting together a small crew consisting of Grayson, Anya, two diviners and two warrior mages. You will be the seventh member of that party. You will be on call 24/7 and will be required to rush to the site of each new dust sighting. You will guide your teammates in the basic world. And you will answer directly and only to me."

"I'm still in," I said. "It will be an honor to work alongside Grayson, Anya and the rest of the collection crew."

"We'll call ourselves the collectors," Grayson said.

"Cool," I said with a smile. "What else do you know about the dust?"

He held his hands apart and formed a circle with his fingers. Inside the circle a new hologram of the dust on a glass slide sparked to life. "In the chronochambers we have a working theory that the dust causes a delay in the DNA replication of cells in the victims. It's as if they are caught in two times at once which stuns their cellular activity. Think of it as if they have been suspended in a cocoon sewn together with a trillion tiny glitches."

The reality of that struck deep. I didn't want to imagine how that felt for the victims, the anguish of being torn apart by time. I got a taste of that in the time vortex—the difference was that I had a chance to fight while Faion and my mother and the others were helpless.

"Messing with temporal shifts is kind of our turf," Anya said. "You mess with it, you mess with us. If anyone can decode and reverse-engineer the dust process, it's the chrono team."

Grayson squeezed Anya's hand. "I will lead the crew with Anya as my second." There was a natural warmth between them. Anya and Grayson were much more than colleagues, they were together in every sense.

"Chronomasters have been banned from the basic world," I said. "And not for no reason. Are we sure this is a good idea?"

Among the rarest and potentially most disruptive mages, chronomasters were restricted to the Deep Down. The consequences of accidentally halting time in the up above could be irreversible and devastating.

"Desperate times," Helianna said.

"There are no guarantees," Grayson said. "Any new substance we create to negate the silver dust's effect may come with its own dangers."

Anya nodded. "We all need to keep that in mind."

Celia looked at me, finally. "Those of us who have a

personal interest in finding answers quickly must proceed with patience, as much as we want to rush and save the ones we love."

The tears in Celia's eyes drew tears from mine.

"The Lunar Order teaches patience," I said. "As long as it takes to get this right and end this nightmare, I'm all in."

"Good. We have a team of seven. Your mission starts now," Helianna said. Her exhaustion made it hard to determine if she was pleased.

Anya squeezed my hand. "Welcome to the collectors," she said.

Helianna picked up her scroll and walked out.

Grayson circled the table to pat my back. "The entire crew will meet at the main chronochamber at 4:00 pm sharp."

I nodded. "I'll be there."

Grayson took Anya's hand, their fingers intertwining. She whispered into his ear as they left. It was nice to be reminded happiness was possible.

"I knew you want to be involved," Celia said. "I am sorry that I had to betray your trust to make that happen."

She was right, but I felt agitated. Sometimes it felt like everyone and everything was trying to get a piece of me.

"Don't worry, Miss Celia," I said. "You made the right call. I need to be doing something to help."

Celia's lips spread into a warm smile. "You seem troubled, Luna."

Her smiles always had a disarming effect.

"They think I'm immune. Yet, no one thinks that's odd."

"You're hardly the first lunar witch to have a special resistance to dark magic. That's why Immortals have long feared your Order. It's also why they have hunted your kind in centuries past."

I guess I knew all that. It still worried me that a hyper methodical, by-the-book mage like Helianna would raise zero questions about it.

"There's someone who wants to be here," I said, having almost forgotten.

"Someone? I'm sorry, dear, I don't understand."

"Cyrus McDonnell," I said. "He requests a temporary seat on the Board."

Celia arched an eyebrow. "I'm going to need more than that."

"He's the leader of the local pack. They have three shapeshifters in a coma thanks to the dust."

Celia considered my words. "The Alpha of the San Diego region asked you to advocate for him? How does that happen?"

"A long story, but yes, he did. And I know my word holds little weight, so I'm asking if you would convey his plea to Helianna? She might consider it coming from you."

"A shapeshifter Alpha sitting at the highest Board on the West Coast," Celia said as if talking to herself. "That's hard to imagine."

"Desperate times," I said, invoking Helianna. "I'm sure

you know that shifters often work in high-level research in the basic world. They're hunters, in every way possible, and Cyrus knows the terrain of the San Diego region better than anyone on Earth. He offered his full hunting instincts to the mission as well as the help of some great shapeshifter scientists."

Celia studied me like she thought I was on drugs. "A werewolf bit me once," she said. "He bit me right on a nerve center. It hurts to this day."

I stared at her, my hopes dropping quickly.

Celia sighed. "I'll talk to Helianna. She'll think I'm crazy."

"I know it's crazy," I said. "I really appreciate this. If she could just mention the idea to the Great Chanter."

"Whoa," Celia said, her eyes narrowing. "You're really invested in this."

"I just don't think we can turn away help."

Celia stood. "I'll see what I can do."

She touched my shoulder and turned to go.

"Miss Celia, one more thing," I called after her. "If someone wanted to get information about a chief necromancer, where would they look?"

She smirked and shook her head. "I'm a diviner and I never have a clue what will come out of your mouth next."

"I think my grandmother would agree with you."

"Iris is proud of you, young lady, but I'm not a fool. I know you mentioned her to make me feel a certain kind of way. Grandmotherly, let's say."

"Did it work?"

"It most certainly did not," she said.

"My request is part of a—"

She lifted her hand to stop me. "I don't want to know, and I was always going to tell you because I trust you."

"Thank you."

"The Central Museum of the Lower Realms. Ask to see the ancient scrolls and look for the *Seventeenth Almanac of the Melded Ages*. And think before you act. That last bit was for your grandmother."

MY HEAD SPUN AS I hurried down narrow passageways in the Education Sector. This place was amazing. Magical script in all the world's languages, from old to new, from Sumerian to Ancient Egyptian to Afrikaans, was engraved on the walls in scarlet and gold.

I arrived outside the ornate double doors of the Central Museum. My heart pounded in my chest as I stepped through the etheric scanner and signed in at the reception desk.

"Where do I find the ancient scrolls?" I asked.

The clerk smiled and led me through aisles until we reached the ascending platform. She adjusted a dial and then left me. The platform was a marvel of sliding gears and plates that silently ground against each other like the moving pieces of a medieval clock fueled by magic. I stepped onto the first plate. The platform whirled and dashed to the right, then upwards, then downwards until it locked into place outside the Almanac Section.

As soon as my feet hit the floor, a seven-foot troll blocked my way. He was dressed in a green woolen vest and pants. His round wire frame glasses slid down his baby eggplant nose and he pushed them back up.

"None shall remove items from the Almanac chamber," he said, his jaw shifting awkwardly as he spoke as if it was cracked and had not yet healed. "The secrets of the chamber shall remain secrets of the chamber."

I nodded. "I am aware."

"Penalties start with a six-month ban from the Museum and..."

He noticed the pin on my lapel that Helianna's assistant had given me. It gave me unlimited access to archival artifacts, no questions asked.

The troll grunted in disapproval. "I am here if you need assistance."

He stepped aside and let me pass.

I decided to find the *Seventeenth Almanac* on my own to hide my intentions as much as possible. After a few wrong turns I found my way. In deference to the book's age, I gently set the heavy Almanac on a desk before carefully opening to the table of contents. I found no obvious reference to Cerber. Unfortunately, that meant slowly turning every page manually—all 3,238 of them.

I scanned page after page, searching for any mention of necromancy. It was on page 1,874 that his name first appeared: Cerber the Eighth, Chief Master of the Necromantic Order and Changer of Faces, the Darkest of the Dark who had been offered a drink from the Immortal spring when he beheaded all six heads of the Great Kerverous, a weredog larger than a cave bear. Kerverous had ransacked through the Eternal Halls and the Divine Chambers wreaking havoc and feasting on the mounts in the Eternal stables.

The Immortal spring water had prolonged Cerber's life to at least ten times that of a normal mortal. The images of him were small and blurry, but there was no doubt that Cerber could alter his facial features to match any age he wanted.

According to the Almanac, Cerber had been an expert in both martial and dark arts and a General in the largest army of undead ever to walk the Earth.

Cerber's undead army had defeated the army of the Eternal Boronin in 1142 during a dispute over a mortal woman.

I rolled my eyes. Was this the Trojan War sequel? Will men ever stop warring over a woman? I mean, seriously?

Cerber's power had grown so extraordinary he managed to behead the great Boronin. He then proceeded to stick the severed head inside a jar filled with arsenic, salt and vinegar so the Eternal couldn't regenerate his body. He kept him like that for 48 years before an alliance of Eternals and Immortals managed to locate Cerber's enchanted castle through an abandoned portal and free Boronin, who was never quite the same.

Cerber was not found in the castle.

I turned the page again and the walls closed in on me. I stared at his name in print. I felt the desire to run. Horror's name featured right next to Cerber's. After Boronin's liberation, Horror intervened on behalf of Cerber to convince the Great Eternal Magistrate, aka Preceptor of Gods, to allow him to capture and rehabilitate Cerber on the condition that Cerber pledge allegiance to the First Council of Eternal Beings and surrender his rule over occult magic.

When Horror himself was found guilty of sedition and was confined to his chambers for his attempt to alter the flow of time, Cerber reclaimed his independence, turned renegade and entered the gates of the dark magic realm where he had reigned since. The only silver lining was that, according to the almanac, Cerber could not return to the basic world.

The passage on Cerber ended with a referral to the Apocryphal Archives.

"Always with your nose in a book."

I turned around to find Gram. A big ear-to-ear smile broke out on my face as I fell into her arms.

"Gram, how's this possible? Why are you here of all places?"

She brushed back my hair. "I'll never betray my sources."

"You have one source, Gram," I said. "I've missed you so much."

"Oh, my dear heart, no matter how much you've missed me, I've missed you more. The young move swiftly, the old are weighed down by sentiment."

"I'm just happy you're here. Even if I did tell you to stay put."

"You should never scold your grandmother."

Uh oh, lecture time.

Gram took on her most vexed expression. "Sophie Collinsworth, what foolishness has you volunteering to be Helianna's dust collector?"

I guess grandmothers share everything. "Did your source tell you she suggested me for the job, Gram?"

"She left that part out," Gram said, not pleased. "She will be getting her own earful."

Take that, Celia! Now Gram's coming for you.

"Tell me, careless child, why does it have to be you, a young witch who has chosen a normal life? There are mages and witches and sorcerers with decades of experience in the Deep Down."

"You know all about silver dust?" I asked.

Gram nodded. "All now know, young and old."

"Helianna's convinced I'm immune to the dust."

"And if she's wrong, my granddaughter will end up suffering the same fate as my daughter."

I tried to smile for Gram. "That won't happen. I promise."

She shook her head. "You can't make that promise," she said, becoming suddenly fragile. "If anything happens to you, I will never forgive Helianna. In fact, I might even brew up a few unpleasant spells for her."

Did my Gram just go full gangster right now?

"Shush, Gram. This is my choice, not hers. And don't be turning anyone into a rat, no matter what happens."

"I won't," she said.

"Or anything else, Gram!"

She sighed. "Fine, but now we'll have some tea and cookies. I have some Oregon gossip I've been saving." She knocked some lint off my shirt. "Stay with us in the DD a little longer, Sophie. We'll have a girl's night."

"Sure, Gram, of course. I'd love that."

I felt calm and hopeful for the first time in days. That was Gram's true magic, making me whole. With her there with me in our ancestral realm where the happiest days of my childhood took place, I felt at home.

My real home.

Chapter 15

Something nipped at my big toe. With my eyes still closed, I straightened the blankets over my legs and turned to my side, facing the wall. Seconds later, someone breathed on the back of my neck—a short, quick whine with some low growling mixed in.

I jumped and sat up on the bed, a ball of light flickering in my hand. The perks of the Deep Down. You could use as much magic as you pleased, and nobody batted an eyelash.

A large, four-legged creature stepped inside my light. Its long snout dripped snot. Bright red eyes stared at me, un-blinking. My throat constricted. The grimy fur on its back was a mess of tangled black curls studded with twigs and pebbles. Its fangs were the size of my thumbs.

The black demon stared me down. The light in my hand morphed into an energy bolt. As dirty and foul as it looked, the beast was odorless and completely devoid of an aura. It was as if its essence had been entirely stripped away.

The hound sat back on its hind legs and lifted an enormous paw. A piece of crumpled paper was stuck there.

I snatched the paper and reluctantly lowered the energy bolt. The hound relaxed and began licking its paw. I turned my attention to the message.

Outside the portal there waits
every woman's dream, patiently.

If that didn't prove that Chaos was the Lord of the Black Demon Hounds, I don't know what would.

The hound got up and headed for the door. I grabbed a blue cardigan I had borrowed from Gram and followed him out. We went through the quiet village streets of the Deep Down with the fairy-tale little houses and blooming front yards, down winding staircases to tunnels illuminated by flickering magic lanterns.

The hound's paws hit the ground silently, the outline of his body an iridescent shadow as he trotted ahead of me. If not for his heavy breathing on my neck earlier, I'd have thought he was no more than a specter.

We reached the portal guard post. The guards were missing. I threw a cloaking shield around myself and the dog and proceeded with caution.

The hound came to a halt in front of an old portal that was rarely used as it had exhibited unsteady energy in the past.

I chanted the magic words to get us both through.

The night air outside was crisp and calm. The moon was two days away from full. I drank in its silver energy.

"The moonlight becomes you, cupcake."

The demon dog ran to Chaos who leaned back against an incense cedar, grooming his fingernails with a clipper.

"Heel, you ugly mutt," Chaos said, scolding the excited hound.

"Sending me a demon dog could have blown my cover."

He grabbed the dog by the scruff of its neck. The beast whimpered. Chaos tossed the hound aside. The beast vanished before it hit the ground.

"What dog?"

"Cute trick," I said. "Can I go back to bed now?"

"Is that any way to treat the man who traveled all the way to this sweaty cauldron of fettering witchcraft to revive your friend?"

I studied his bent expression. "Is this more of your nonsense?"

"It's the art of discourse," he said. "That thing that your beloved basics have sacrificed at the altar of all your precious devices."

"Okay, boomer," I said.

"What was that?" he said. "Some insipid catchphrase?"

Not telling (but yeah).

He peeled himself from the tree. The moonlight flashed through his open coat and shone bronze on his powerful pecs. He wore no shirt under that coat.

I was tempted to reveal that Penelope had told me he was the successor to Darius and Lord of the Black Demon

Hounds. I decided not to push because whenever I did, he always disappeared into a puff of blue smoke.

"Very well," he said, sincerely. "I am here to assist you with the fate of your diviner. We can bring him back, together, if we combine our powers."

I glared at him. "If you're messing with me, I swear..."

He grinned. "You put such weight behind your threats like an angry bird. I respect the delusion in that. If your desire were a weapon, you would be as powerful as you will need to be. When all this passes, I may find myself missing that pretty little head of yours."

"My head? Is *that* a threat?"

He bit on a fingernail. "A feeling. You wanted it straight."

"What?" I said, shaking my head. "No. No more feelings."

He spat out a sliver of fingernail. "What's it going to be, Luna? My time is precious. If you want to save the diviner, we have to go in now before the sun comes up."

"Why? Are you a vampire? Or is it only your powers that melt?"

"I'm good 24/7, but my planner is full up for tomorrow."

Every word he said felt like a lie, but my gut told me he was not lying about healing Faion. In any case, he was willing to try. Did his reasons matter? Did the hidden price that would assuredly come matter?

"Yeah, okay." I walked to the portal and scanned the energy around it to make sure it was stable. I turned to Chaos. "Don't make me regret this."

He joined me at the portal. "Isn't regret what you do best, silly witch?"

I closed my eyes and exhaled through my nose. "Around you? *Yes.*"

"Shall we proceed?" he said.

"The portal is heavily warded against Immortal essence. You'll have to stay close if we're to enter together while I neutralize the spells. Once inside we'll need a strong invisibility spell."

He made an impatient gesture. "I can hack your bloody wards," he said. "How do you think the death doggie got in?"

"The hound doesn't have Immortal essence and you cloaked him and..." I realized I didn't know how he did the last part. "How'd he get in without the magic words?"

Chaos winked. "I gave you a taste the other day."

He hugged me to his chest. I could feel his pulse thumping in my ear. Everything spun, including us, in a frenzied whirlwind, smoke blurring our surroundings.

When the spinning stopped and the smoke dispersed, we were standing on the inside of the portal. I felt a little sick.

"How do you do that? How do you teleport through wards? How do you teleport across the planet?"

"Mystery is the spice of life, moon kitten. Maybe it's illusion, maybe it's mind over matter, maybe I dance with time like your Chronomaster buddies."

Dude knew everything. Beyond annoying.

"I just realized," I said.

"Realized what? That you should cook me dinner one day?"

"That you like me and you're not sure that's a good thing."

He raised his eyebrows condescendingly. "Oh, naïve child, don't take this personally, but I haven't liked anyone since the bronze age."

"And you hide behind jokes. I do that, too. Must be a family thing," I said. "How are we related again?"

He covered his ears and began humming... *Beethoven's 9th Symphony?*

"Keep it down," I told him. "The spell doesn't really make you invisible, it's light refraction that keeps people's attention off you, but all is lost if they can hear you humming Beethoven."

"I think your yapping mouth is the real liability."

He had a point. We had just passed by the guard post when a male voice boomed behind us. "Halt!"

I turned, slowly. A young guard stood at ten feet from us, red headed with an open, honest face. An electric net sizzled in his hands. An electromancer. If he threw that net at us, we'd get fried on the spot.

The guard motioned me with his chin. "Please, step aside."

"I don't understand, what's going on?"

"Move away slowly. There's a cloaked entity standing

by your side."

I did my best to chuckle in a convincing manner. "I think I would know if I had an invisible stalker."

Chaos exploded out of the misty cocoon of invisibility. He grabbed my hand and spun me, light on his feet, humming Sinatra's *Fly Me to the Moon*.

The guard tensed. The red-hot net in his hands hissed. "This is your final warning. Step away from the witch and identify yourself."

Chaos released me. His anger was palpable but so was something else—his magic core pulsed through his skin and nipped at me, knocking me back. I'd never felt anything as potent as what was coursing through him although *why I could feel it* was the spooky part. Our connective life forces rattled me.

"I feel your terror, little man," Chaos said. "You hold your lasso like it's a toy. Did you forget your cowboy hat, son? This is grown-up business. Now run home to your momma. None but me will know your true heart."

That's not helping, Chaos. If he provoked a fight, we'd be screwed.

Instinctively, I thumped my foot and immediately tapped into the ley line that ran underground.

Bingo. The raw energy responded and shot upwards, knocking the electric net out of the guard's hands and dis-integrating it.

Chaos pounced, putting the electromancer in a headlock.

I fixed Chaos with my hardest glare. "Hurt him and your balls are next."

Chaos glided his palm over the guard's face. "Fucking humanist," he muttered under his breath.

The guard's body went limp. Out cold.

Chaos set him carefully on the floor. "Gentle enough for you?"

"Did you do the memory wipe thing?" I said.

"Is that a serious question?"

We entered the Infirmary through a side door. The hallways were dark and eerie like in a horror story. Our footsteps echoed unnaturally loud.

Faion lay on his back. His face wasn't calm or peaceful—it held the expression of someone going through shock.

Chaos tossed the covers aside and placed his hand on Faion's chest. "The poison has dug in," he said. "It would take days to extract it the right way."

"We don't have days," I reminded him.

"No, which leaves us the nuclear option."

"Do I want to know what that means?"

"It means it's good we're immortal, because we can absorb most of the impact and survive, but we all, him as well as us, may be forever impacted."

"Don't care," I said. "I'm ready."

Chaos flicked his wrist. The door closed. Raw energy sizzled out of his hands. "Fighting off necromancy is a brutal feat," he said. "You will be my buffer, Luna Mae. Your job is to keep the energy circuit from overflowing, keep it contained in this room, by letting it stream through your body."

I didn't dare ask questions. They'd be answered soon enough.

Chaos let his magic spill into the room in a cascade of yellow light. A dome formed above us, cloaking the magic scene from the outside.

He opened his arms. A surge of power knocked the wind out of me. I struggled to keep my bearings and stay on my feet as it kept coming.

The brunt of the energy hit Chaos and pushed him to the ground, all the way down until his face and body pressed hard against the tile surface.

My muscles numbed as I absorbed more energy that invaded my every cell. I gritted my teeth. The fight was just the beginning.

Chaos struggled back onto his feet. He summoned more of his power and he let it pour inside the dome, enveloping us. His veins and arteries and tendons bulged with the over-saturation of the force inside him.

He fought his glowing fists from pulling him down before his hands leapt up onto Faion's chest. A raging tidal wave channeled through Chaos, through his arms and into my friend's body.

My insides twisted into pure agony—a screaming emptiness and throbbing dread compelled me to give in, to let Chaos's excess of power explode like a nuclear bomb.

Shit, the nuclear option. That wasn't hyperbole.

The energy kept flowing, hissing into Faion's very core. I closed my eyes, imagining how the magic ripped through his organs, replacing damaged cells, connecting tissue, sealing leaks, chasing the damned poison until it burned.

Blinding discharges of energy escaped the sizzling circuit between Shadow Warrior and untested Mist Rider, shooting upwards to ricochet off the ceiling and rain back down on us, encircling us in a warm, green haze.

Then it all ended.

The magic died. A sudden icy breeze blew in when our protective dome disintegrated. I shuddered. Chaos dropped to his knees.

Deep within, I felt as if someone had torn out my magic core and scraped it raw. With trembling knees, I threw myself onto the edge of Faion's bed.

Faion's eyes were still shut, but his face muscles had relaxed. His chest rose and fell more steadily as he took in deeper breaths.

Tears rolled down my cheeks. "Faion." I gently shook him, then took his face into my hands. "Talk to me, Faion. Please."

His eyes blinked half-open and closed again. I felt pangs of relief and panic pulsing through my lungs.

Chaos lifted his head and turned his sunken eyes on me, trying to smile through exhaustion. He was depleted and sweaty. "No necromancy. Our power was enough." He said it softly as if awaiting applause.

"Thank you, Chaos," I said through tears.

He held onto the bed to climb to his feet. "Keep your thanks, my biscuit. Better you remember this moment when we meet again."

I knew there'd be a price, but I was too happy to care.

"Chaos," I said. "What about the others? My mother?"

The bastard was too tired to laugh. "I really must be going. You are more foolish than I thought, mist maiden, if you think the reckless use of ancient power you just witnessed can ever be repeated."

He begun to spin. The smoke gathered at his feet.

"I'll be forever grateful," I said.

Smoke snaked up his legs. "Forever's a long time. I'll sleep three days to recover. Make sure the world survives until I wake."

I watched the blue smoke fade after he was gone.

Faion's eyes fluttered. I took his hand.

"This can't be," a voice said behind me. I knew it was Celia.

She stood inside the doorframe, hand on her mouth.

"Come," I said, offering my hand.

"I sensed my boy calling me. I didn't dare think it was true."

I smiled. "It's true."

Celia walked to Faion. "By what miracle?"

"I don't know," I told her. "I found him like this."

All the lies were weighing on me. I wanted so much to

speak the truth, now and forever, but I couldn't. No one would understand.

Faion opened his eyes.

Celia kissed his hands. "Oh, little mister, can you hear me? Can you hear your own grandmother?"

Faion licked his lips. He blinked a few times, slowly. Then the corners of his lips curled into a weary smile.

Joy erupted everywhere inside me. Tears flooded my cheeks. I had no idea how much repressed regret, pain and worry I had smothered away in the deepest parts of me just so I could get out of bed in the morning.

"Bless your troubled soul, my precious boy," Celia said through her pain and tears. "This happiness is a gift." She turned to me. "I don't know how, but I know it wasn't free. I shall not forget this gift, dear girl."

"Faion is a gift to us both," I said.

"He'll need rest and nourishment," Celia said, eagerly. She took one of my hands into both of hers and kissed it. "Go, Luna Mae. You can't be here. You were never here. It's not yet your time."

I nodded. In a daze, I did what she said. I left. I trudged down the eerie corridor, past the other rooms with more poor souls stuck in time, past my mother's room. The tone of Celia's voice whispered in the shadows.

Not yet my time?

What did she mean? What had Celia seen?

Chapter 16

THE TEXT FROM EMMET had come while I was taking my shoes off at my apartment right after I fled the Deep Down. Cyrus had some vital information he wanted to share and would meet me downtown at the Hybrid Workout Club, a small gym owned by the pack.

After a quick shower, I put on my activewear and headed out. It was a while yet before lunch, so the gym was nearly empty. I kicked at a punching bag, waiting for Cyrus to grace me with his presence. Maybe if I burned through some adrenaline, my mind would slow down for a few minutes.

Faion had sat up this morning and even though he was still too exhausted to hold a conversation or eat solid food, the healers at the Infirmary expected him to make a full recovery.

I attacked the bag with more spinning kicks, then hammered it with combination punches. I pushed myself beyond my normal limits to try to shut down my brain and become fully physical, fully animal. I hadn't worked out since Europe and vowed to get back to honing my body with rigorous workouts to help relieve stress and ready myself for battles to come.

Sweat poured down my face, back and chest. I took off my long sleeve workout top and bent forward for a hamstring stretch. I sensed someone's gaze on my backside. I rolled up and looked around.

A woman wearing a head scarf peered through the window. Her vacant gray eyes locked on me. She was tall with sharp, angular features.

As soon as Cyrus stepped in the gym, the woman bolted away.

I realized that Cyrus was checking me out. My wine color crop top and leggings were standard gym clothes, but to invasive male eyes revealed most of my feminine lines.

"You're in decent shape," I heard him say, "but there's a few areas where you need some muscle work to firm things up. You'd have a hard time keeping up with many of my clients."

No filters when he spoke. Alphas for you.

He walked to the boxing ring with the slow grace of a lion waking up from a nap. He wore a blue crew neck gym shirt and gray mesh shorts, a white towel wrapped around his shoulders.

"You're a physical trainer," I said. "If all your clients are who I think they are, nobody can keep up with them."

Cyrus donned a satisfied grin. "I train all kinds. My female middle-aged basic clients could kick your ass in this ring."

He bent down and slid under the ring ropes. "Let's go, college girl. Join me," he said. "Free lesson."

I took the boxing gloves hanging from the ring post. "You said you had information for me?"

"Such a one-track mind," he said.

I'm trying to save lives, not watch you flex, bro'.

"Not here for banter," I said.

He danced around the ring, punching the air. He had a professional boxer's perfect form, balance and strength.

"Okay, I respect that," he said.

"I kept my end of the bargain. Your plea has been made to the Board. You'll have your answer soon."

He leaned on the top rope. "Soon would have been yester-day."

I raised an eyebrow. "What happened?"

"Last night. A pack of hyena shifters in Merida were at-tacked. The word coming down is that none were spared. We haven't seen anything like this. They are comatose at best. Maybe dead. Lost to this world. They all had families."

My heart started racing. "You say all... how many?"

"Twenty-seven. There is so much dust still on the site that no one has dared to get close enough to search for survivors."

I felt cold all over. The attacks were accelerating. "What a nightmare. Cyrus, I can help with that search."

He stood up. "You? How?"

"The Board has assembled a dust collection crew. I'm on that crew."

His eyebrows came together. "No offense, but why would they include a low-level witch with no leverage or expertise?"

I shrugged. "I was standing there. Wrong place, wrong time."

"Nah. Bullshit. What offense did you commit to be put at such risk?"

"They think I'm immune. My friend was a victim and I got near the dust in the aftermath. I survived. Probably dumb luck, but now I'm a guinea pig of sorts."

He took a moment to process my story. "Aren't you just full of surprises, Sophie. That's the name you use in the basic world, right?"

Nice try, but no way I'm telling you my magic name.

My phone vibrated. I motioned him to wait.

"Hello?"

"*Your place is warded*," Winter said.

"Don't break my damn wards," I whispered into the phone. "It took forever to put them up."

"*I can break them, then rebuild them enhanced.*"

"Let them be. They're mine, I like them."

"*Where are you now?*"

I looked at Cyrus, then covered the phone so Winter wouldn't hear. "The guy on the phone, you should really talk to him."

"For what reason?" Cyrus said.

"He's a… friend… a Seventh Council Magistrate and very invested in beating the dust."

Cyrus tried to keep his face as still as a boulder, but the red sparks flashing in his irises gave him away. He was stunned.

"Yeah, I trust you," he said, shrugging. "Tell your *friend* to come over."

"Jonas?" I said into the phone.

"*Who are you whispering to?*"

"Come meet me at the Hybrid Workout Club down-town?"

"*A gym? I thought you didn't like to sweat.*"

"Just get down here."

I had no more patience. I wanted Winter's input and it wouldn't hurt to hear his impression of Cyrus. And maybe the alpha shifter would learn some humility when faced with the Alpha of all Alphas, the Shadow Warrior. I mean, you don't have to try so hard when you're already the alpha.

Cyrus lost all interest in talking after that. He moved over to the free weights. Judging from the number of 45-pound plates he benched, his strength was almost mythic.

A touch of magic tingled my stomach as Winter entered the gym, dressed casually and seemingly in high spirits. His eyes greeted me with blue sparks.

Cyrus returned the bar to the rack and bounded over, his skin and hair glistening with sweat.

The men glared at each other, saying nothing.

Testosterone anyone?

I stepped between them. "Jonas, this is Cyrus McDonnell, the head of the local pack. Cyrus this is Jonas."

"The Immortal Magistrate," Cyrus said.

Winter kept silent. Given the animosity between shapeshifters and Immortals, especially after the savagery of the metamorphic night, I probably should have warned him he was about to meet with a pack alpha.

I spoke fast. "Cyrus's people were hit with the dust. They already had three in a coma when Cyrus requested a seat at the Board's meetings and now an entire hyena pack was wiped out in Merida. The Board has yet to decide. He's offered to put the pack's considerable resources and hunting expertise at our disposal."

Winter clenched his teeth. "Why would a pack leader want to subjugate himself to the stuffed shirts on the Board of Supernatural Orders?"

It talks!

Cyrus didn't miss a beat. "I have over five-hundred shifters yapping for blood, that's why. And if you heard the girl, we've lost people. Better question, why would an Immortal bother himself with the problems of us lower supernaturals? And are you really at the beck and call of a weakly witch?"

Are we done flexing, boys?

Winter snorted. "The witnesses from Merida, where are they?"

"There are none," Cyrus said. "There's dust everywhere.

The slightest breeze makes a dead zone for a hundred yards in every direction."

Winter nodded. "The original three, were they hit individually?"

Now Cyrus nodded. "One by one while they were in town. We have barricaded the main pack keep and our smaller remote locations. We're keeping a 24/7 watch, but we don't have fancy wards or any other kind of magic to protect us from supernatural attacks."

Winter's icy demeanor melted. "Yeah. We'll provide protective wards as requested and directed."

Cyrus stepped forward. "On behalf of the San Diego Pack, I accept your offer and would like to express our gratitude. A recompense of your choice will be offered in return. It would be our distinct honor to do so."

Winter shook his head. "No need for that."

Cyrus opened his mouth to insist but changed his mind. *Smart.*

Winter grabbed my elbow, ready to leave.

"Maybe I should go with Cyrus," I suggested. "I can make sure the wards are put up around the compound perimeter."

I sensed Winter tense. "The pack keep is a large construction with towers, underground cellars and even panic rooms. I'll send someone far more equipped to get it done quickly and correctly and to set down wards strong enough to keep intruders out."

"Truly obliged, Magistrate," Cyrus said with a slight bow.

Jonas considered Cyrus. "My expert will be there by nightfall."

Did he really shut me down in front of Cyrus?

As we walked away, I felt Cyrus's eyes on me. I looked back and saw him leering at me, an eager smile on his face.

Thought I wasn't fit enough? Men, sometimes.

Outside, I stepped into Winter's path. "Did you really have to make me look like a foolish girl? You're no better than him, always trying to prove what a big man you are. I'm so done. I'm done."

His disapproval broke out all over his face. "How exactly did you get mixed up with alpha shifters, Luna?"

Did he not hear a word I said?

He nodded. "Your wolf boy, yeah? That's it, isn't it?"

"That's hardly the point, you psycho. Cyrus is now a key ally."

He snarled. "A key ally? Really? If that steroid jackass ever gets so much as a tiny whiff of how ancient and strong your magic is, he'll hunt you to his last breath."

I laughed. "Let him try. I'll swat him away like a fly."

"Except there'll be 500 flies with fangs, coming from all angles."

"Good thing I'm not yours to protect," I said, fuming.

Winter sucked in his breath. "The tactless creature was nearly in heat looking at you. He would do anything in his power to sweep you off your feet, so he can use your magic to expand his territory. It's his primal objective. He's done it before. More than once. Shifter and fae royalty, daughters of ancient families, all swept off their feet so that Cyrus can grow his power. The list of the women that have visited his bed chamber is a mile long, and they all brought with them new alliances. He'll treat them well as long as they're useful and not one minute longer."

"Really? Interesting. He must be good in bed. Thanks for the tip."

I thought his head would explode.

"Relax, you total idiot," I said. "I'd sooner sleep with you. That's how little I want to sleep with him. That dude is so obvious and inappropriate. I had zero interest before you said he eats women and spits them out in his dungeons."

Those words didn't please him either.

"Come on, did you really think I'd fall for an egomaniacal, power-hungry alpha-hole who wants to use my magic to advance his own agenda?"

Too close to home? Oh, the irony.

He was speechless.

This is fun.

"Give me some fucking credit, Jonas."

"Shifters are smooth seducers," he said, punching every syllable. "Even your little wolf toy with his sliver of expe-rience almost got you. If you're turned off by Cyrus that's because it's his first move. He's infinitely more nuanced than pup boy or you for that matter. Stay clear, understand? He knows a hundred ways to catch his prey. Believe me."

I chuckled. "Oh my god, you're jealous."

"Don't ascribe base human impulses to my pragmatism."

Our eyes connected for a long beat before we continued walking.

"Shit, I have to alert the crew," I said.

"Luna?"

I turned. "Right. I was going to tell you. I'm on this dust collector crew that Celia recommended me for because I'm immune. There's a few of us on it, including two pretty chill Chronomasters. They're actually a couple. It's cute."

I started to walk, but he grabbed my wrist. "This is a job for Immortals."

"What? No, I'm a collector. I agreed."

"We're going. The others are not immune. And we're going to Merida the fast way."

I wavered. If anyone could help me it was Winter, but I had agreed to work within the boundaries of the crew. By even mentioning the crew to others, I had already violated the first rule of *Dust Club*. On the other hand, there was a ton I was still keeping from Winter—the blood note, the Rotunda, Cerber, my summoning of Chaos—really, when I thought about it, it was a whole shit show of secrets. I wouldn't even know where to start.

"But I'm a collector," I said, batting my eyelashes. "Fine. You win. And by the way, where the hell have you been all this time?"

"Doing detective work," he said. "Eternal warriors have

been sent out through the south equinoctial observatory." His face became rigid. "They haven't been out in two thousand years."

I was almost afraid to ask. "Why now?"

"They're hunting," he said.

"Hunting what?"

He wiped his lips. "Something terrible... and immense."

Chapter 17

THE ANZA-BORREGO LEY LINE spewed us out where it intersected with the Merida ley line. That line extended east all the way to Havana. I wondered if Immortals could ley-ride underwater and how that would feel.

We landed in the middle of an onion field. I fell forward onto my knees, clutching my stomach. I felt sick and disoriented.

Winter knelt next to me and rubbed my back, gently. His warm hand moved up and massaged my neck. My nausea subsided.

"Will it always be like this?" I said, out of breath.

"Depends." He paused. "How often you do it, but after a decade or two it gets better. In a century it will be as easy as taking a bus."

A century? I'm out. I'll fly commercial.

"What now?" I said. "No more ley lines."

"Now we walk to the hyena camp."

We walked through fields and past stone ruins. I quickly became overheated. There was something abnormal about the high temperatures. Winter took my hand. His touch cooled me every time I felt the heat rising. Last time we traveled via the ley line express, Winter had used a misty breath to shield me from the arctic cold of Northern Alaska. He said he was the man in icy climates. Apparently, he was the man for all seasons, a one-man thermostat.

We were headed toward Hacienda Sotuta De Peon. According to Cyrus, the attack occurred a mile south of there.

"Isn't the Mayan city of Chichen Itza around here?" I said. "Maybe we could stop by after we collect the dust."

Winter creased his brow. "The feeble mindset of the young... you're immortal, Luna, come back on your own time."

Okay, maybe it wasn't the best timing for sightseeing, but did he really have to be such a dick every chance he got? I let it pass because a strange sensation in my chest started to take hold, as if my magic core had begun leaking.

We rounded a corner on the path and came upon a collection ditch at least ten feet deep and thirty feet wide. Small bird and animal carcasses topped heaps of rancid garbage. Hyenas were notorious for such medieval waste disposal practices.

"We're not far now," I said.

Winter pulled me to him. "There's a disturbance in the ether," he said under his breath. "Dark magic happened here not long ago."

We took slow, deliberate steps as we scanned the horizon. My energy tingled in my fingertips, but something was off. It felt unstable and disconnected.

A new foul odor reached my nostrils, an acrid stench, putrid and undefinable, that had been masked by the trash and rotting flesh.

I had to hold my breath, repulsed.

Winter crouched as we reached a boulder stained with blood. Behind the boulder and partially covered with brush, a monstrous and malformed body lay curled on its side.

The face was caked in dried mud and blood but was undeniably human. Patches of mutilated fur covered the arms and legs of the beast through tattered fabric. The feet had human heels, but the front half were brown paws with sharp claws in place of toes.

The stomach was torn out, a gaping dark hole left in its stead. I gasped. A jagged blade had wreaked havoc on the victim's chest and gut.

The mangled body belonged to a hyena guard who was slain while trying to shift. The expression of utter shock on his battered face mortified me.

Taking a shifter by surprise was no small feat. All their senses were sharpened, and some believed they even had a sixth sense. Their hearing was supersonic, and they could take off like rockets when they sensed danger.

"Do you feel that?" I asked Winter. "The pressure in your magic core?"

Winter stood up. "Yes. It's exponentially stronger than the other times I was in close proximity to the silver dust."

"That's because there's exponentially more dust."

In the distance, no more than three hundred feet away, the hyena camp came into view as a cloud of smoke lifted.

"This is where robust shields come in handy," Winter said.

No, really? It's not like you've told me a dozen times.

A blinding metallic sheen flashed from the camp like the sun reflecting off a great silver sea. My stomach clenched. Everything in me resisted the idea of getting any closer to the poisonous substance.

"No one is entirely immune to the dust," Winter said. "Not Shadows. Not Mist Riders. Certainly not at this volume. We'll be affected, but we'll be strong enough to survive it."

I was not convinced, but I was grateful I hadn't called the collectors. There would have been no way to protect them from this deluge of toxicity.

"Do you have the boxes?" I said, even though I knew the answer.

He tapped his satchel. I could hear the clink of titanium.

We took the path to the camp. My magic stabilized as Winter's shield encircled us both. It was like a soothing breeze blowing inside me.

I readied myself for the onslaught of sinister energy to

come. I began to make out the first bodies in the distance, sprawled unnaturally on rough terrain, completely mummified in silver.

Winter stopped. He took a sharp breath in. "Run!"

Run? Run where?

"Which way?"

Too late. The ground cracked open beneath us. We were sinking into quicksand. By instinct I tried to latch onto the nearest ley line.

Nothing. There were no ley lines and no magic sources available from without or within. Just darkness and grains of sand filling my mouth.

WHEN I OPENED MY eyes, the white light was so strong I had to squint. I was in a strange, eerie reality—everything was painted with an unnatural chalk white, from the floor to the walls to the ceiling.

Winter was crouched with his back to me. He tapped the white floor, then glued his ear to the wall. He was stripped down to his shorts, glistening drops of sweat all over his torso and arms. His breaths came quick. His golden skin stretched over his tense muscles.

"Is this my coma?" I said. "Am I stuck between time?"

The Winter creature spun around. He had savage eyes.

"Are you a phantom?" I asked.

He grunted. "Luna, you're awake."

"Awake? Was I asleep? Are you really here?"

"We're both here," he said, standing up.

My gosh. This has to be a fantasy.

"Your body was overwhelmed," he said. "It couldn't handle the intensity of the etheric transference during teleporting."

My heartbeat accelerated. His voice came from inside me.

He returned to searching along the wall with his fingertips.

I took in a deep breath. The chamber was rectangular, or at least I thought so. There were no openings, no doors, no windows. The walls connected to the ceiling and the floor seamlessly like everything was one.

I tried to sit up, but the room started spinning. I stayed put. "Teleported?" I said, trying to understand. "Why did you let me sleep?"

Winter shrugged. "You needed the rest and I've been busy looking for some flaw in this energy blocking cell."

I had trouble following. "What are you talking about?"

He grabbed me under the arms and propped me up against the wall, placing his balled-up shirt under my head for cushion. "This room is designed to block out all magic and disconnect us from natural energy sources. We are rendered basic here, powerless."

"That's not possible."

"Go ahead," he said. "Search for your magic. Access your

energy sources. Search within your core. Search for mist magic."

I closed my eyes and did as he said. I couldn't feel anything. Not a tingle. I panicked. I couldn't locate an energy current coursing through my veins. I searched for ley line points and lunar energy and found nothing at all.

"It's all gone," I said, terrified.

"We were led into a trap," Winter said drily. "The whole thing was a fucking ruse."

"That bastard Cerber," I said through clenched teeth.

Winter arched an eyebrow. "Cerber? What do you know of Cerber?"

"I think he's the Lord of the Soul Swallowers," I said. "When you were gone, he sent me another blood note. He said he'd exchange Faion's life for mine if I met with him."

"Good thing you're smarter than that."

I bit my lip. Guilt gnawed at me, but belated explanations and the blame game wouldn't help us now.

"It could be your gym buddy, Cyrus," Winter said.

"What? Explain the logic on that one."

"Well, he did send us straight into the trap."

"He sent us to where his people were massacred."

He had no answer for that.

"Never mind," I said. "Let's just find a way out of here."

He returned to his wall, exploring it with both hands now.

"Any weak spots, Sherlock?"

He shook his head. "Whoever built this neutralizing

reactor knew what they were doing. It's without a flaw."

Suddenly I felt paranoid. "I can't be stuck in here when people are out there being wiped out by the dust. People depend on us, Winter. You're a Shadow Warrior. Do something! You're a zillion years old. You've seen everything. Come on, use your tricks! Where's that brutish rage?"

"Are you done? I've already tried all that," he said. "Even the rage. You've been out for hours."

I studied our all-white cell. The whole room began to feel as constricting as a straitjacket.

"I wonder, do you think there's silver dust in the walls?" I said.

"I think nothing. I got nothing."

"Break them."

He looked at me, uncomprehending.

"The walls," I said. "Even without your brawny magic, you're still brawny in a physical sort of way, aren't you? Don't all those muscles work? Break the damn walls down and get us out of here. Time to be a basic badass."

"These aren't real walls. It doesn't work like that."

"Says who?" I said, then jumped to my feet and started banging on the wall, my fury boiling over. I punched and I growled and kicked, then slammed my whole body against the wall.

He gathered me into a bear hug, holding down my arms. "Snap out of it, Luna, you won't heal."

My breathing came out in gasps. My knuckles were

battered. "We have to find a way," I said. "Don't give up. Try everything!"

"Okay," he said. "We'll find a way."

I stayed in his arms for a long minute. I wondered if Chaos could still feel me, my presence and location. Would he break through these impenetrable walls with his demon hounds to save me?

The seconds ticked by in my head. I could use some water. I wished my backpack had made it through the reactor walls. It hadn't. It was just the two of us.

"How's Chazona these days?" I said.

He tilted his head and squinted at me. "This is what's on your mind? You care about Chazona's wellbeing... right now?"

"I wouldn't say *care,* but since she's your lady friend, I thought it would be polite to ask. I hope she doesn't find you half as annoying as I do."

"My *lady friend*?" He laughed. "And you accuse *me* of being jealous?"

"Don't flatter yourself, golden boy. I feel sorry for you if I'm being honest. Here you are, all ripped with those smoldering deep blue eyes and you have that brooding mystique, and yet you're stuck with the ice queen. Do you need an electric blanket to sleep next to her at night?"

I didn't see it coming. His face went red. By the time his steel grip flipped me over his knees, there was nothing I could do about it. I tried to fight, but he outmuscled me so easily.

His palm smacked my butt three quick times.

It didn't hurt except maybe my pride.

"Your childhood was full of moments where you needed that," he said. "But your people were soft. So now it's done."

"What the hell's wrong with you?" I yelled. "I'm not a child. You can't manhandle me like that. What fucking century are you from?"

"All of them," he said.

"You're the broken one," I said. "You're really messed up. Save that for the ice princess from hell. I'm not interested. Okay?"

"I'm only going to say this once. If I wanted Chazona, I'd be with Chazona. She's not my cup of tea, okay? So, go ahead and retract your little claws and stop imagining some cheap, ill-fated love triangle."

"Huh? *Triangle*? I'm not any part of that. I'm good, dude."

"You don't sound good," he said. "You sound bothered."

We were trapped in a panic room, destined to dehydrate and starve to near skeletal but alive flesh sacks and yet, all I could think about were ways to make his dumb ass suffer *after* we got out of here.

"I saw you kiss her," I said. "Why do men lie all the time?"

He looked stunned. "I kissed Chazona? When?"

"The night you told me to go to Sweden. I came to tell you I was sorry I overreacted. Then I saw you two on the balcony."

"You shouldn't have seen that."

"Well, I did. Busted."

He rubbed his forehead. "You saw nothing. Chazona kissed me and I told her to go home."

"Why was she there that late... a regular booty call?"

He shrugged. "She probably knew you were watching."

I rolled my eyes. "More sick Immortal games. Sounds like a perfect match to me. Winter and his Ice Queen."

"I can't keep up with your schoolgirl paranoia."

"You're such a condescending ass."

He leaned back against the wall and closed his eyes. This was the closest I'd ever seen him to being contemplative. We should be talking about our options, not arguing about Chazona.

I felt tired, drained. When Winter opened his eyes, some new quality was there, *I don't know*, maybe regret or uncertainty.

"I did something," I said, trying to sound nonchalant, "when we were at the Sacred Vault, something I shouldn't have."

He released the deepest sigh. "How am I not surprised?"

"Do you want to hear it or not?"

He bowed and opened his hand.

"It happened in the Eternal Archives during the minute or two I was alone. Right before Chaos lit the match."

He tensed and readjusted his position.

"I found your file. I didn't have time to read much, but I

did read the part about Helen and Christian."

He didn't react. He just stood there, completely still.

"I'm sorry I didn't tell you earlier. I didn't think…"

"You didn't think we'd end up trapped together."

Well, yeah.

"You thought you could keep that secret forever," he went on.

"Forever's a long time."

He sneered. "Truth is you couldn't keep that secret for five minutes. I read it on your guilty face the moment I returned to the Archives."

Oh.

"Since we're being honest," I said. "A child? Why then, after all those centuries? Why Helen?"

He took time to measure his response. "Trying to figure out who you're supposed to be is an eternal burden. It can be overwhelming for anyone, Luna. But for an Immortal the predestined emptiness of eternity, the amassed losses, the constant battles, the never-ending journeys, the dying generations stacking up behind you, the complete lack of permanence for everything but yourself, will snuff out your very identity. I wanted an identity. I wanted what I could not have. It was a moment of weakness."

I hadn't felt a lot of that yet, but I had suspected that all Immortals must eventually learn to live with a loneliness beyond all telling.

"Helen was British," he said.

That astonished me, Winter offering information willingly.

He must be convinced we're doomed.

"We dated for a few months in the mid-fifties in London, where I worked as a New York Times correspondent, before she found out she was pregnant."

"You were a journalist?" I said, ever more shocked by the second.

Did I really know him at all?

"It was a phase. Life among basics. It didn't last. Helen never quite knew my true story. I went by the name Aidan Parsons. I tried many times to tell her, but she was killed before I found the courage." His eyes were haunted.

I touched his hand. His pain seared right through me.

If we were to spend the rest of our days in this place, I didn't want us to be physically next to each other but emotionally alone—I wanted us to spend our days *together*.

"We might never get out of here," I said. "Dying over and over from thirst and hunger while our bodies struggle to regenerate. We need to be together. We can't be at each other's throats, unless maybe we should drink each other's blood to hydrate and regenerate and stay strong."

He chuckled. "My luck. I get locked in here with a vampire."

I laughed, then stopped. "Wait, vampires aren't real, right?"

"Luna, you really have to stop talking, so I can think."

"I can't stop talking when I'm tired."

He took my face in his hands and kissed me.

Slowly, deeply, passionately.

His body pressed against mine and my brain emptied out all my frantic thoughts. It felt good. I wrapped my arms around his neck and pulled him closer. My tongue found his tongue. It felt like we were flying.

He pulled back, flashed a labored smile. A desire to be naked with him, to intertwine our essences, skin on skin, warmth on warmth, until I could convince myself we would be happy here, overtook me.

"Don't stop," I said through desperate breaths.

"I've wanted this for so long," he said, "but it's dangerous, Luna. Our combined etheric essences would be too much for any world to hold."

I giggled. "Show me, big man." I looped my hands behind his neck and trailed my fingernails down his back. He grabbed both my hands, stopping me.

"I'm serious, Luna."

"Jonas, what?"

"When I told you to go to Sweden, it was because of this. I wasn't sure I'd be able to control myself around you."

"And that would be bad, how?"

He released my hands which leapt right back onto his chest.

"You and me," he explained, "we carry rare magic. Our magic is not the same but similar in intensity and ferocity. During sex, the path of energy exchange that would be forged between us could be devastating."

"I'm counting on it," I whispered.

"This isn't a game, Luna. There is no shield and no cloaking spell in the world that could suppress the deafening reverberations of our combined essences. The echoes would reach the Eternal Halls, and the secret of your true nature would be revealed to all. The Eternals would know a majestic union had consummated. They would investigate. Horror would know, too, if his vision is unleashed through Cerber."

I slid down the wall to the floor, defeated. "So, that's it? We can never sleep together?"

He joined me on the floor and kissed behind my ear. "Out there... (*he whispered as he kissed my neck*)... we can't... (*he nipped at my lower lip*)... but in here... (*he kissed behind my other ear*)... we are sealed away, inside an energy vacuum... (*he pushed the neck of my shirt down my shoulder to kiss there*)... away from all things supernatural."

Winter wrapped his thick arms around me and found my lips with his. His tongue was hot and sweet as it swirled with mine. My hands adjusted to the swelling curves of his firm chest.

I planted two kisses on his pecs. He reacted with a soft moan as if a big current of energy gathered inside him.

"Are you sure?" he said.

"A majestic union... I'm beyond sure."

That was true. I had wanted him for so long, I could finally admit it to myself, but now I wanted to disappear in ecstasy. I wanted to forget our fate. It made it sweeter that I had always been drawn to him, in almost mystical and intoxicating ways, beyond the realm of human desires.

He lifted me to my feet and pressed my back up against the wall. "You're so beautiful, Luna. So sassy and delicate." His breath tickled my ear.

And there, in the doom of our eternal prison, Winter kissed me again and again. His muscular body crushed onto mine, pushing me into the wall.

His hand cupped the back of my neck as he forced his tongue deeper into my mouth, yearning to unlock the secrets of my blood.

I curled my arms around his neck, unable to hold back a second longer. He had created a perfect symphony of sounds and sensations inside my body and I wanted to reward him. I wanted to show him how grateful I was.

Our mouths locked for a while, kissing and nipping at each other's wet lips, licking, sucking, devouring. Pure ecstasy coursed through my veins, arousing my most sensitive pleasure zones.

"I don't care if they hear me in the great Eternal Halls. I don't care if the Great Eternal Magistrate comes after me himself," I proclaimed through groans and heavy breaths, because I wanted him so bad and I didn't want him to even think about changing his mind again.

"Do you want to feel alive, to really feel alive?" he said, his eyes gleaming with possibilities and promises.

I nodded, biting on his earlobe gently. "I've never felt more alive."

"No," he said. "Even more than this, the thrill of being really alive. I used to know it, but now I only get small glimpses. Your fresh spirit, your untamed vitality... You've made me feel more alive than I have in many years."

My knees went weak and my senses numb. If he kept saying those sweet words, I'd collapse in his arms. There was something hypnotic about his voice and the way his eyes dug into me, scraping away my defenses.

His hands attacked my shirt and my jeans roughly until he held me naked in his arms. He hoisted me up and I wrapped my legs around him, my hand searching for support on the wall.

I didn't know love making could be such a feast of the senses. We were in complete synch, body and mind. We moved and moaned as one. I didn't want to escape this moment ever, but my body began to surge and quiver. I gave in. Everything imploded in a hot electric pulse. My belly tickled and my mind blew into warm sensations that thrilled every joint in my body. Pure ecstasy lifted me up, rolling through me like a hurricane, leaving me gasping and whining in exhaustion as my heart stretched out and pounded blood into all my arteries and veins.

Winter moaned. Magic rose within me like a sweeping thunderstorm, energy sizzled out of my hands and melded with the translucent energy spilling out of Winter.

What the hell is happening?

My magic core swelled and screamed with persisting force, regenerating itself beyond maximum force. Winter's body quaked as he stretched his arms toward the ceiling and growled with the ferocity of a furious Warrior King, terrifying me, energy streaks running through his veins like blue lightning.

The joy reached an unbearable crescendo... *every single thing was shaking!*

And then the whole world began to crumble.

Chapter 18

THE TREMBLING WALLS PUFFED up like popcorn and then ruptured amidst a cacophony of earsplitting sounds. The ground shuddered and cracked open. Agonizing pain blazed through my magic core which kept feeding on an incessant cascade of energy waves spilling out of everywhere.

Winter took me in his arms. "Absorb as much energy as you can, find a way," he yelled.

In the haze of the magic overflow, his face looked inhuman. Muscles strained under taut skin fighting to contain the energy assault. His veins bulged as he replenished and overloaded his core.

I had barely grabbed our clothes when the walls exploded under the pressure of blinding white energy. Winter clamped me inside a bear hug to shelter me from crushing shockwaves and an avalanche of debris.

We were shot upwards, smashed through the ceiling and kept going. For a few heartbeats, everything went black until we were thrown onto a patch of sand. In the distance, the hyena camp flickered with a silver sheen.

Winter encircled us both in a bubble of shielding energy.

"What the hell just happened?" I said. I handed him his clothes and started dressing. It felt offensive to be standing naked so close to what had become a mass tomb for all those fallen shifters.

His eyes scanned the area with feral intensity. "If I had to guess, I'd say that we created an energy fusion that manifested as an uncontainable surge that inflicted cataclysmic stress on the anti-magic reactor."

I chewed on that for a moment. "When can we do it again?"

The beginning of a grin curled his lips. "Whenever we are in an anti-magic reactor. We found the cheat code."

"No, really," I said. "That's not something I can do just once."

"Luna, I told you, out here in the world, that's not an option. We both have very old, very divergent, raw magic. In a sense, we are polar opposites. Apart, we can control our etheric essences so that the magic stays contained and undetected but combined it would be like a giant asteroid colliding with the planet. The whole world would know, whatever's left of it."

Suddenly, I felt cold. "And did you take all that into consideration before you made love to me?"

Doubt swept over him. "I thought so, I did. I convinced

myself we had no access to magical resources in that box. I thought we'd be safe."

My dry eyes started to sting. "I don't believe you. You had to know something like that was possible. Was it an experiment?"

His eyebrows came together. "I didn't use you to break free."

"You know what," I said. "Don't say another word. I don't care."

His eyes pierced through my disappointment. "I wanted to make love to you, Luna. I've always wanted that. You may not believe it, but I don't have all the answers. I'm sorry, but I've never slept with a mist rider before. I didn't know anything could produce that much combustible energy inside an anti-magic reactor. At least we're free, and we know that it can never be repeated."

"And Winter has another notch on his belt. *Mist rider*, check."

"You process this whatever way you need to," he said. "Make me the bad guy like you always do. I don't care. Our problems are not what's at stake in the world right now. I'm staying on task and I suggest you do the same."

There he is... the unfeeling bastard is back.

"Aye, aye, commander," I said. "Let's fulfill the mission."

"We have to move," he said, ignoring my sarcasm. "Mind your every step. There are likely more traps to come."

"Then we should leave," I said. "They have our number. I

doubt they even care if we collect more dust."

"Yeah, maybe," he said, "but it's our only play."

"It's their play, not ours."

But it was too late, he was already plowing ahead without me. I followed close behind, making sure I stepped in his tracks.

Winter found his satchel. The titanium boxes were intact.

Every step brought us closer to the silver strewn terrain. The musty air felt heavier and more toxic. Winter fortified our shield.

The hissing force field he created was so charged with electrical current it made my skin ache. I threw a shield of my own on top of his.

He glanced at me, unimpressed. How I wished now I would have taken his advice and practiced my shield skills more diligently.

We reached the first traces of dust on the ground. There was only a handful of it where we stood but enough to irritate my throat. Even with the shields and our cores overfull with magic, the silver dust tasted like poison, slowly scraping off layers of my very essence.

I choked. Winter's aura fought against a gray wisp of smoke. I was sure mine didn't fare any better, probably worse.

He kneeled, reaching inside the satchel to bring out the two boxes and a titanium scoop. Next, he reached outside the shield and filled his scooper with silver dust. The skin on his forearm melted, exposing raw flesh.

Winter gritted his teeth. He poured the dust in the titanium box. As soon as his arm healed, he repeated the process. Every time he collected dust, his arm burned, he waited to heal and started all over again.

It was a slow, painful process for us both. We moved around the periphery of the camp, crouching, pouring a constant stream of energy into the shields. The fatigue was overwhelming. Every now and then I felt like falling asleep, the result of expending too much magic too fast.

Finally, the boxes were filled. I locked them and Winter put them carefully into his satchel. I released a sigh of relief. Then I saw them.

A legion of demonic beasts lined up along the camp's perimeter. They glared at us through coal button eyes. Clumpy green slobber dripped down from their misshapen snouts and drooling fangs.

Old friends. Dust monsters.

I grabbed Winter's hand. "They can break through shields."

He nodded. There was recognition in his eyes. He picked up the satchel with the dust slowly, then scooped me up and ran off.

A pack of monsters broke away and scampered towards us. Their feet were flat and not ideal for high speeds. Their wet bodies wobbled as they ran into each other. One of them fell and was trampled over.

Without hesitation, Winter jumped over the first wave and kept running.

They charged after us, their howls a maniacal song from Hades, but their speed was no match for Winter.

He suddenly came to a halt. I had assumed his plan was to run all the way to the ley line, but instead he dropped me roughly. I rolled onto the ground.

Winter unstrapped the satchel.

"You okay?" he said.

I nodded. He had run just far enough from the silver dust so I could breathe freely again.

"Keep moving," he said. "They want to drag us into the time vortex."

Out of nowhere, two blazing swords popped up in Winter's hands. They were blades of pure fire. I sprang to my feet and bounced around.

The monsters closed in, heavy tongues hanging out of their mouths.

Power burst from my own hands, yellow spheres of lethal current.

"Kill them all," Winter growled. His voice was so eager for violence it made me wince.

He flung himself at the dust monsters, slashing, gutting and burning his way through them, making a Mardi Gras of innards and severed limbs.

A second wave of monsters stampeded their way to Winter. They threw themselves at him, dozens upon dozens of them, like they were pouring out of the ground, until he vanished completely under their weight.

A group carved away from the rest and shot out at me.

Keep moving, keep moving.

I swirled on my feet and released my yellow current, letting it cut clean through the midsection of three monsters. Claws grazed my skin, fangs nipped my hair, but I kept dancing, light on my feet, hurling scorching energy.

Winter exploded from underneath the dust monsters, dripping with thick brown ooze as he removed heads in his fury. Another wave of monsters arrived.

I stomped my right foot on the ground, calling onto the ley line energy. The earth tore apart, the gap widening with incredible speed.

I pulled at the ley line, creating an enormous magnetic field that pulled monster after monster into the gap. When the last one had vanished, I reversed the field so that the ground closed, swallowing up the last squeals and howls of the crushed monsters.

My heart jackhammered.

I checked on Winter. He was busy removing demon guts and green slobber, but I didn't give a fuck. I ran to him, jumped up and wrapped my legs around his hips as he hoisted me into his arms. I kissed him like he was about to disappear. If this was the last time we could share a kiss, I was going to make it count.

Chapter 19

THE GUARD LED ME down fifteen flights of stairs to the very depths of the chronochambers, an area that was off-limits for everyone except the Chronomasters and now the collectors. He unlocked the door and left. I took a seat in the small anteroom and placed the titanium boxes on the side table. A collection of clocks studded the walls, covering the entire span of clock history: from sundial clocks to the first mechanical clocks to atomic clocks.

A strange knot squeezed my insides. We were running out of time. Every clock agreed with me.

A heavy door barred the way to the main chronochamber. Made with a compound of both basic and magic metals, it was infused with spells and reinforced with wards. Behind that door, a series of experiments had been conducted covering all facets of the space-time continuum. For now, the rare technology and witchery of the chambers had been diverted for the exclusive purpose of understanding and defusing the silver dust.

Last night had been lost to nightmares about the white room. Again and again, I slipped into the energy-stifling cocoon and tried to dig my way out with bare hands until nothing was left but bloody stumps in place of fingers.

A dozen times I ached to call Winter and ask him to come over. A dozen times I had changed my mind.

I told myself I had to pull the bandage off quick to get over it. I could not depend on Winter for comfort. Our paths would soon diverge again after we brought down Cerber and destroyed the silver dust. He had repeated so many times what was best for us, and I never wanted to hear him say it again.

Footsteps approached. I straightened my hair and took a deep breath.

Grayson walked in, followed by Anya who gesticulated behind his back.

"You don't get to have an opinion on my wardrobe, big guy. I'll wear a tiny leather skirt and a strapless top just to teach you a lesson."

Exasperation laced Grayson's face. "We're not going dancing, baby. We're going to war." He turned to me with pleading eyes. "Please, Luna, explain to this naïve mage that the purpose of our ascending to the up above is for official business as representatives of the Board of Supernatural Orders, not going to a fashion show."

I stared at them at a loss for words. "Let her wear whatever she wants," I said, exhaling hard. "What's the big deal? Although, you might not have to visit the basic world after all." I took Anya's hand. "But if you want, I'll convince Helianna to let us have a girl's night in San Diego when this is over."

Anya's eagerness deflated. She belonged to a magic order who were never allowed to leave the Deep Down.

Grayson furrowed his brow. "Luna, what happened?"

I slid the boxes across the table to him. "They're both full of silver dust."

The Chronomasters stared at the boxes without blinking.

"How is this possible?" Anya said.

"I received a tip about a huge dust attack in Mexico. I was told no one had been able to get close. The toxicity was through the roof in every direction. I wanted to check it out before putting everyone's lives at stake. I barely made it out in one piece, but not before I collected that."

Grayson's face burned red. "You just went without so much as a consult?"

I nodded. "I had to trust my instincts. If the crew had come, you would all have perished. If there's not enough there, we can take the crew on the next hit if it's smaller and more contained. I hope that's enough, to be honest, because I don't want to ever see another scene like that."

A vein pulsated in Grayson's temple. "You violated every rule of the collectors. Every single one, Luna."

Sorry for saving everyone's life. Sheesh.

"Okay, well, I could always take it back," I said. "Or I am

sure other research units would love to take a look."

Dude, I nearly faced an eternal prison to collect this!

Anya hugged me. "Don't listen to Grayson. He acts like a brute, but deep down he's a softie. He'll probably cry with joy after you leave."

Grayson smirked. "I'm tough enough when I need to be," he said. "But Anya's right, I am very excited to have these samples. And I have great respect for the courage and valor necessary to collect it."

"See what I'm saying?" Anya winked. "Eventually, he gets it."

He tries to impress her, and she likes to tease him. Cute.

I bowed, slightly. "It was my honor to deliver this to you. I have faith that you two lovebirds will now find a way to save our world."

Anya hugged me as Grayson put on his protective gloves.

FAION SAT IN AN upholstered rocking chair by the window, eyes fixed on the trees outside. He had been moved into a renewal villa where patients spent the last days of recovery before being released.

His vitals and his complexion had returned to normal. They had been loading him up with nutrients and forcing him to sleep. He looked completely serene and introspective. When he noticed me standing inside the doorframe, he lifted his eyebrows and gave me a half smile.

I hurried to his side and hugged him tight. "You're never leaving my sight again. That almost killed me," I said.

"Kingdoms rise and fall, stars get pulverized into black holes, but Sophie Collinsworth keeps it all about her," Faion said.

"That was mean," I scolded him. "You must be better!"

"I don't know what I am," he said. "I'm still kind of not here."

His words broke my heart.

I pulled a chair to sit facing him. "One day at a time, okay?"

"If one more person tells me that."

"You can't rush these things."

"I'm totally fine," he insisted. "If it were up to me, I'd already be back at my place chilling with Joey."

"Well, it's not up to you. Besides, San Diego is a mess right now."

He bent his face at me. "That shit happens when you happen."

I shrugged. "And yet you love me."

"That's only because I'm stupid," Faion said.

"Hey, I'll take any kind I can get."

Faion smiled, then leaned to me. "Do you know how Joey's doing?"

"He's fine. A little confused, probably, about what happened, but I know you'll find a way to smooth that out."

"He needs to dump my ass. I would. I don't play."

"Well, it's a good thing he's a better man than you then, because he was ready to fight to protect you from us."

"How'd that pudding head of yours get so clear and confident? Sounds like some girl got her cobwebs cleaned out from you know where."

How the hell did he guess that?

"I don't know what you're talking about," I said, blushing.

"You don't, huh? You going to tell me when you're ready."

"I want to hear about you," I said.

He regarded me with joyless eyes. "I honestly didn't think I'd escape the dust. It felt like endlessly drowning and choking, but without a throat, without a body even. Just crushing loneliness and desperate suicidal longing."

Despair drove its ugly little teeth deep into my chest.

His eyes turned glassy. "Everything and everyone faded. I felt hunted by the silence, which was trying to swallow me, become me—it wanted to erase me, make me nothing, a soundless scream in a void."

I listened hungrily, trying to force myself into his place in that lingering, agonizing panic. A sudden weariness overtook my senses. For a moment, it struck me that my life had been nothing, a blank space, that everything that happened to me so far was inconsequential and pointless.

"You can unpack all that eventually, piece by piece, but now let us celebrate what's most important. You're back.

You're back, Faion."

"True," he said. "And how exactly did that happen?"

Here we go.

"Life's great mysteries," I said. "Maybe you had less exposure. Maybe you're a badass."

He rolled his eyes. "Or maybe I'm friends with you."

"Little old me," I said. "I'm just a girl."

"You a *gangsta* girl who's not to be trifled with," he said. "I know what you are, Luna Mae, and it's fierce and dark and fools should run."

"I'm trying to get to the next day is all."

He nodded, then ignored me. "There was someone in that hospital room. I never saw him. I felt him. A demon with two burning red eyes ripping through my ribcage and clasping onto my heart. I thought he'd kill me for sure, tear my heart out and eat it. I was so afraid I wanted him to do it. I wanted it to end, but then he started sucking the poison out of my blood, drop by drop to feed his own bloodstream. He poisoned himself to save me."

I stood and leaned against the window, choking on deceit. "That sounds like one of your visions."

"No, it doesn't. It was no vision. And you know that because you were there, Luna, tugging at the demon's strings, making him do your bidding."

"Right, my pet demon Spot," I said, looking outside. A palette of soft oranges and purples painted the undersky. "There's darkness and there's light. I'm me, that's all I can be. I'd do it all over in a heartbeat."

"Will you let me finish?"

I looked down to him.

"You fought for me and I love you for it."

My eyes watered. "You better have loved me before then."

He smiled. "Facts, but to be straight... that was you, right?"

"Are you taping this conversation?"

"Nah, but it was you. I know it," he said. "Your secret's safe, but that other secret's not safe, the one about you going to the love rodeo. Go on, girl. Speak!"

Chapter 20

THE NOTE WAS NAILED to my door with a golden dagger. I waved my hand across the width of the door. My wards responded, humming and flickering.

There were no irregularities in the etheric charge around my home. There was no lingering essence at my apartment, friendly or otherwise. I closed my eyes to focus on any disturbances in the earth energy below. All good. Coast was clear except for the necromantic message pinned to my door with a dagger.

I grabbed a handful of tissues from my purse. I didn't want to touch an instrument oozing with dark magic. I patiently wrapped the tissues around the golden handle and pulled, catching the note as it spiraled downwards.

Setting the dagger aside, I unfolded the note.

You have some interesting friends.

That was it. No signature, no puns, no instructions. It

made the sparse message all the chillier. Did it refer to Chaos saving me at the Rotunda? Or was it a veiled threat against Faion, Lily, Lucia, Tam?

I unlocked my door and nudged it open. Everything was in its place. I stared down at the dagger. There was no way I'd bring it inside, but I couldn't leave it outside the door either.

I dropped my purse on the couch and fetched an empty trash bag from the kitchen. I used the bag like a glove to pick up the dagger and hide it under the sink. I'd have to ask Celia or Penelope how to dispose of an evil dagger.

I closed the door and leaned against it. The toilet flushed in the bathroom. My body turned ice cold. Energy sizzled on my palms.

The bathroom door opened. A man walked out drying his hands with a towel. He was under six foot, chubby around the middle and completely bald. He wore tight black jeans, a studded black jacket and a spiked leather collar. His round, freckled face emanated a relaxed malice.

My pulse accelerated. The man was Cerber.

I hadn't felt his presence, I hadn't sensed his etheric essence and the wards were intact. How did he manage to get in?

A flash of sunlight made me look up at a man-sized hole in the ceiling. He came through the roof. Setting wards up there had never crossed my mind.

It wouldn't have mattered. No wards could have held back a dark sorcerer of that caliber.

Electric impulses tingled everywhere. He was real and he was here. Banned from the basic world or not, the Chief Master of the Necromantic Order stood in the middle of my apartment.

"Aren't you forgetting something?" he said. "The knife was a gift."

I slowly crumpled the note in my hand. He could take his bloody dagger and shove it right up his dark sorcery ass.

I raised my chin. "Where are your uglies?"

He carefully folded the hand towel and placed it on the table. His hands were well-manicured like he had never worked or fought a day in his life.

"No need," he said. "They get a little hyper."

I was stalling. I was no match for Cerber. He could move through any world undetected like a ghost. He could bypass any ward, any security apparatus. His powers came straight from Horror. How do you fight powers when you have no idea what they are exactly?

"Are the wards yours?" he said. His voice possessed the cultured curiosity of a well-educated man.

"Who wants to know?"

"We're playing this game, huh?" he said, almost disappointed. "So be it. Let me introduce myself. My name is Berend Van den Berg, also known as Cerber the eighth, Chief Master of the Necromantic Order and notorious General of the Undead Legion."

I'm Sophie, recent San Diego State graduate. Hi.

"The wards are mine," I said.

"They're not bad, considering your true age is 23."

How flattering. HoHdhkhdkhadWhat girl wouldn't blush when receiving such a conditional compliment coming from a sadistic autocrat who commands an army of dust monsters as well as legions of soul swallowers?

"Is that what you do? Collect the ages of your victims?"

His expression hardened. "I have heard of this victim culture in your basic world. It presumes one has no agency whatsoever over their own fate. Rather bleak outlook, don't you think? I am not here to kill you, that would be a complete waste of a pleasing specimen. I will neutralize you. Nothing more."

I shrugged. "You can try."

"There may be a season for that," he said. "One must have patience, for we can only live one day at a time. How about we settle for a chat?"

His eyes scrutinized me. I backed away, readying for combat.

"When you listed your titles," I said, "you left out *Changer of Faces*. Your face can take on any age you like. Your soul swallowers have the same ability."

He grinned. "The schoolgirl has done her homework."

"Or, you wanted me to notice, so that I could find you."

For the first time he hesitated. "And yet, you didn't run scared to hide out in your subterranean catacombs. Do you have a death wish, Luna?"

I didn't run because you were banned from this world, you asshole.

His face boiled and blistered, turning red as the top layer of skin melted. His cheeks hollowed out, deep wrinkles creased his forehead, age spots ravaged his hands and face. A hundred-year-old man stood before me.

I clapped. "Impressive. You look pretty frail. Maybe this is my chance to take you down."

"I would be a hard elder to abuse."

A charge of elemental energy escaped my hand. It collided with an invisible shield and exploded into tiny colorful sparks that fell to the floor.

Cerber's muscles twisted, his skin stretched and his back straightened, changing back to the middle-aged man who had broken through my roof.

"Just a test," I said.

He circled me, flaring his nostrils as he sniffed at me.

I'm so over dudes circling me.

"Quite fascinating," he said. "You still don't know who you are."

Trust me, I know plenty, but I'm not about to compare notes with a psychotic villain.

"Does anyone ever really know themselves?" I quipped. *"Each is the farthest away from themselves."*

He raised his brow. "Nice party trick, quoting German philosophers."

"You seemed like a Nietzsche man," I said.

Being outmatched in magic, this stalling effort was my only reasonable tactic. I kept trying to work out what, if anything, could penetrate his shield.

His manicured hand reached out to take mine. When he closed his eyes, a hostile wave of magic invaded every cell of my body like electricity.

Clenching my teeth, I zapped his hand with just enough energy to pry open his fingers and pull away.

His eyes flew open. "Yes, yes. Horror will be most interested. You'll make an excellent bargaining chip."

Trying to keep my growing nausea in check, I spun on my feet and struck his shield with everything I had. He reinforced the shield on the fly, creating bubbles of energy streaked with a full spectrum of colors.

His face strained. For a moment, my energy had cracked his shield. He instantly mended the force field, but I saw what I saw. He wasn't infallible.

Cerber clapped back with a staggering energy wave. I dived to the ground to avoid being pulverized.

He sighed. "I preferred talking but okay."

I climbed back onto my feet as dark energy spilled out of him and whipped around the room. Tendrils of smoke spread from the walls like the branches of a dead tree. I ducked and threw a shield around me. The dark energy ricocheted off my shield and punched an apple-sized hole in the wall.

My wards growled.

From a crouched position I hurled a bolt of energy at Cerber. He deflected easily, sending it racing back at me like the return of a tennis ball. The force knocked me back off my feet. I skidded across the carpet, my shield flickering.

By now, I was quite pissed. Stirring energy clenched my insides, wanting to strike out. A thin beam of energy turned into a sweltering whip. I hit him with it so hard my hands tingled.

Cerber grabbed the tip of the electric whip with his bare hands. Any other creature would have been barbecued on the spot. Cerber yanked the whip to him and me with it. My feet slid across the floor. I let go of the energy whip which caused a surge that sent me flying and shut down my shield. My back smashed against the wall. I heard a bone crack.

Cerber leapt into the air and landed next to me like a cat.

There was pure malice in his glare. "Is that all you got, sickly witch?"

A clawed hand of black smoke cut through my re-emerging shield and gripped my throat. Its fingers felt like coiled barbwire tightening around my neck. I gagged and gasped for air.

The dark power expanded all over the floor. Dread enveloped me like rotten flesh. Smoke crept under the shield. I couldn't move.

Cerber snapped his fingers. The smoke stopped spreading, giving my panic a short break.

"Work with me here," he said, feigning concern. "If you

surrender to my will, the pain will end."

I fought to get the words out. "I'm not giving my soul to the devil."

"And that will be your undoing. You need sharpened survival instincts to win a battle against superior magic. As it is clear you haven't inherited those from your progenitors, someone should have taken more time and provided you the chances to acquire those skills through experience."

His hold on his magic relaxed while he talked. He eased his grip on my throat. I focused inwardly. Power rushed to me from my core and liquefied the dark clouds of smoke pinning me down.

Rage twisted Cerber's face. "I'm trying to be reasonable with you for your own good and this is how you repay me?"

His body stretched towards the ceiling. A dark light painted his face, making him appear like the negative of a photograph. He was beyond seven foot tall now.

His voice boomed. "Tell me, how did you escape the time vortex?"

Cerber waved his hand to gather a storm of smoke around me.

Talking hurt, but I couldn't help myself. "Fuck you."

The barbwire grip tightened. I lost access to my energy, like I had been wiped clean of magic.

Cerber grew angrier by the second. He had become a demonic giant. "And how did you break out of the inverse energy reactor?"

Oh, it has a name.

"Is it because you're the witch who is no witch?"

He was running out of lines faster than a guy at a bar.

"Spell out the truth of what you are," he insisted. "Admit to yourself that you are a great and terrible weapon."

"No!" Fire was dissolving my insides into a hot liquid.

"I'm being gentle," the madman went on. "Say it and I will show leniency. Say it not and your suffering will become unimaginable."

I opened my mouth to say something. Words wouldn't form. The giant crouched, his face drawing near to mine. The deadly grip abated.

"Just say the words," he whispered.

I quickly spat on his face.

His face became a bestial mask. "The dagger on your door, that is Horror's own dagger. He himself forged it. A long time ago, he presented it to me as a gift. It is the rarest of weapons for it can end immortal lives."

Cerber dashed to the door in a fury.

I stomped both feet on the ground one after the other. The slumbering ley line came alive, reacting to my summon. Raw energy channeled up my legs.

He yanked the door open. No knife. He turned and raised his hand. The dagger ripped its way out of the trash bag and flew out from under the sink, right past me and into Cerber's open hand.

Oh, shit!

Puffs of mist rose from my skin, encircling me in a steamy white cloud.

Cerber caught this out of the corner of his eye.

"Witch!" he hollered. He charged, the dagger shining gold in his hand.

The mist wiped away the smoke claws from my throat. I breathed in.

Come to me, motherfucker.

I struck Cerber with the fluid mist magic that flooded my core. It gushed out of me in waves of staggering force. Cerber's knees buckled, his body vibrating as if being electrocuted, as he shrunk back to his normal size.

The necromancer collected his power with a deafening scream. He reached his arms out to me, desperate to break free from my mist.

Everything hurt, my own magic scraping at my core like a burning iron. Cerber gained ground on me, getting close as he pushed back with a cyclone of dark energy.

Sudden steps echoed outside.

Chaos entered the doorframe. My head imploded with a crushing ache as he broke down my wards.

A red aura spilled from him as he absorbed the ward energy inside his body. I'd never seen anyone walk through active wards so readily. Even the demon beast Cerber had to crash through the roof.

Cerber turned slowly to face the intruder. His face went pale like he had seen Death coming for him. His lips parted into a forced smile. "Her dance card is already full, I'm afraid. Run along back to hide in the shadows."

Chaos faltered. His hand stroked the handle of his sword, but he didn't draw it out of its sheath.

Cerber's eyes teased. "Ah, it's the witch again. You can't stay away from her, can you? How pitiable."

Chaos regarded Cerber with murder in his eyes, saying nothing.

I was completely spent and out of breath and trying to replenish my core as fast as possible.

"Into what spider hole have you stuck your head?" Cerber went on. "Eight centuries is a long time for a man of your skills to fester away like a forgotten, isolated maggot."

Still, Chaos did not move. What the hell was happening?

I struck Cerber with a glowing sphere of elemental energy. He blocked it with a brand-new shield he forged on the spot.

He fixed two hateful eyes on me. "Another time."

Cerber shot upwards and flew out through the roof.

What? No! Total bullshit.

"We could have had him," I yelled at Chaos. "That's the second time you just let him walk. What the fuck? He'd be vulnerable against us both."

He avoided my eyes. "No, he wouldn't."

It hit me that Chaos was scared, and he had no clue what to do with that feeling. I had seen Cerber's weakness. What exactly did Chaos know about the age shifting asshole that I didn't?

My anger welled. I didn't even know who I was mad at… Cerber? Myself? Chaos? Winter? I needed a spa day with Lil so bad! Immortal men were every bit as infuriating as any other type of men. Worse, actually. And now I'd put myself out there again for Cerber or anyone to know exactly what I was.

Chaos couldn't even lift his eyes.

What the F, dude? Snap out of it.

"Can I just have a minute?" I said. "I need a minute. Go get a coffee and come back in an hour."

Without a single word or even a glance, Chaos yanked me into his arms, held me so tight I couldn't breathe and engulfed us in that fucking blue smoke.

Where's that Immortal killing knife when you need it?

Chapter 21

WE LANDED IN AN unfamiliar room. Teleporting felt like being in a tornado of lemon slices swirling in hot water. It made my eyes sting and my skin simmer.

The room looked like a basic study with a desk, two filing cabinets and two bookshelves stacked with hardback volumes. A twin bed had been thrown in to turn the study into a temporary guestroom. The décor lacked any nuance or personality. No one ever wanted this room to feel welcoming. A half-open door led to a small bathroom.

"Where are we?" I said.

Chaos peeked outside through the blinds. "Somewhere safe."

I picked an empty candy wrapper from the bed. "Is this where you bring your conquests?"

The hard glare in his eyes told me I should drop it.

"We have to warn Winter," I said. "He must know Cerber has broken out of his dark realm."

"I don't think so, buttercup. I put my ass on the line time after time to keep you safe, but you just don't listen."

"So what? You're going to be my babysitter now?"

"No need."

He flicked his wrist. Threads of red energy flickered along the walls. Chaos had fortified the room with wards so ancient they might have been Neolithic. A whole bunch of them, hostile and suspicious, whirling about the room in uneven patterns. This wasn't a room—it was a jail cell.

I tried to anchor my sensors inside one of the wards and nearly got my brain fried. The magic fueling them was too primitive yet incredibly potent.

Chaos meant to imprison me here.

This day just keeps getting better.

"Is this your panic room?" I said. "How many women have you brought here? Does kidnapping make you feel in control?"

He shrugged. "Most don't make it through the etheric transference. It's an utter bore dealing with the splattered brains. I'm seriously considering giving it up. Thought I might try torturing animals for a nice change."

I cringed. "Just don't try comedy. Your humor sucks."

"Consider this a timeout. You asked for a minute, well you get as many as you need until Looney Luna is ready to start making better choices."

He headed for the door.

"The wards won't hold me, you know," I said. "And you're

the looney one if you think I'm going to just let you walk out that door."

He turned and showed me his teeth. "You think you can stop me?"

I cracked my knuckles, preparing myself for battle.

He walked to me.

"Stop right there," I warned him.

He kept coming.

My hand sizzled with an electric bolt.

Chaos stopped in his tracks. A deep purple rippled in his irises. He winked, snapped two fingers and uttered one word. "Sit."

The ground underneath my feet shook. A mighty spasm gripped my spine, forcing me down. The room blurred and my knees buckled.

I held onto the desk, fighting against a gravitational force. My mouth opened, struggling to form a sentence. The three-letter word kept repeating inside my head like a metronome. *Sit.*

The urge to comply with his order mounted in my stomach. I was compelled to obey and no matter how I fought it, I was going to lose the battle. I gave in. I plopped down on the bed, cursing under my breath, my limbs shackled by invisible restraints.

"There," Chaos said. "That's a better girl."

I glared at him. "What magic was that?"

"It's my gift of blood to you. After the transfusion, my

blood became your blood, but, big spoiler, it still answers to me," he said. "I can command it as I please and through it, you."

This... Isn't... Happening!

I strained to speak. "Did you know that when you gave me your blood?"

He grinned. "Do Russians drink vodka?"

"Maybe it works both ways," I said. "Maybe I can command your blood."

He patted me on the head. "Good luck with that. I saved the diviner, or did you forget? You owe me."

I had let him get too close. He outmaneuvered me at every turn, and now he had too much power over me. Winter had warned me of this.

Winter. He had to have known I would be compelled to obey Chaos once his blood ran in my veins. Why didn't he say something?

Chaos slapped his thighs. "I'm going to skedaddle. Enjoy your sanctuary until you're mature enough to have a real conversation."

"Screw your sick games. Let me go, Chaos."

"If I let you go, you'll be dead within days, maybe hours."

"Tell me how that's your business."

"Don't be tedious, Luna Mae."

My temper flared. "You may be scared shitless, but I'm not. There's a fight raging out there for the soul of the world and I'm not going to run away."

Chaos had already turned and now he walked out the room. The wards closed ranks behind him, forming a dense, impenetrable wall of energy.

I tried to get up, but not a single muscle moved. I'd have to use every inch of my willpower just to get off this bed. How pathetic.

The truth became apparent. Chaos thought of me as a commodity, a long-term investment, an insurance policy. He had tired of the volatility of my freedom and now he was going to do what, in his mind, he should have done from the start—restrict me, reshape me, reposition me, so he could maximize his asset and realize his advantage. It was not Winter who wanted to use me for his personal gain as Chaos had tried to convince me—it was Chaos himself.

I didn't know how this would end, but I did know I would skin Chaos alive if ever given the chance.

Minutes dragged by. Hours crawled. All I had to show for it was that I managed to shift my position enough to lie down.

Chaos returned with a tray and set it on the bed. There were freshly cut strawberries, a ham and cheese omelet, and a bottle of water.

"You've been resting," he said. "That's good."

"Did you prepare that?" I said, truly curious.

"Are you asking if I can cook? After twenty centuries, you should not be surprised. There were no drive-thru lanes or restaurants for most of my life."

He snapped his fingers and fixed his eyes on mine. "Get up."

Blood rushed to my limbs. The leaden weight that held my knees locked lifted. Something eager and defiant rose in me, vitality returning to my organs.

I stood up and stretched, glaring at Chaos. "Big mistake."

"You can't go through me, little soldier, so take a breath. I will release you after I deal with Cerber."

I laughed. "Really? You'll deal with Cerber? You? Like you did in the dark realm? Or in my apartment? The way I remember it, he mercilessly taunted you and you just sat there and took it."

Chaos's eyes dropped. "Everyone's a critic."

A thunderous echo rolled through the building.

Chaos pounced and ran out of the room. I followed him to a narrow corridor. His sword leaned sheathed against a console table. He grabbed it with one swift move before running down a staircase to a small living area.

The front door burst open. Magic boomed in my ears, deafening me, as the wards collapsed. Chaos raised his sword. I readied my energy. Kirsi darted through the door and crouched like a cat. Behind her, Winter waltzed into the room like a Viking, veins pulsing in his neck.

They took my breath away. *Wow.*

Chaos laid his blade on his shoulder. "Oh look. It's Lord Beefcake and his murderous maiden Kirsi."

He really thinks he's clever.

Kirsi pounced. Chaos met her blade with his.

"Put that sword away," Kirsi said. "Or I will sheath it in your ass."

Chaos giggled happily, then charged and thrust. Their dueling blades clanged loudly.

"Kirsi, fun's over," Winter called out. His command reached her while she was airborne. She twisted to land with her back to Chaos, pivoted away and cursed in Old Norse. She was panting, her eyes darting wildly. I had never seen the deadly side of her before, the *ready-to-ride, ready-to-die Valkyrie.*

Winter put a hand on her shoulder. "Find your peace."

Kirsi lowered her sword and spat.

Chaos kicked a chair hard at Winter who ducked just in time. The chair crashed against a wall and broke into pieces.

Chaos threw a lethal glare at Winter. "How did you find us?"

"If you're chief magistrate of an immortal council, you best know the location of every safehouse of every friend and every foe," Winter said.

It was getting dark. Winter clapped his hands. The light came on. He closed the distance between us and pulled me to his body. He put his chin on top of my head as I buried my face in his chest.

"The day has been a long one," he said, exhaling deeply. "I arrived at your apartment and found it wrecked. It smelled of dark, ancient magic and..." He motioned Chaos. "Him."

"I'm sorry," I said, clutching him tight, needing to feel his physical presence to make sure I wasn't dreaming. "I made stupid choices. I should have waited for you. I confronted Cerber and then he found a way into our world. Cerber came to my apartment. He wanted to offer me up to Horror."

Deep creases striped Winter's forehead.

An animalistic snarl ripped from Chaos's throat. He lunged at Winter and tossed him up against the wall, his forearm pressing on Winter's throat.

Chaos spat out a torrent of vulgarities. "You ball sucking, son of a Nordic whore, fucking goddamned thick-skulled, naïve rube!"

Winter's aura became visible around him, deepening to a smoldering purple. A surge of concentrated power spilled out of his hands.

The energy field blasted Chaos off his feet and crashed him back into a tall bookcase. The entire Encyclopedia Britannica crashed onto his head. Blood spurted from a deep cut above his eyebrow. Chaos scrambled back onto his feet and charged right into Winter, tackling him.

I just about had it. Two demolished living rooms in one day!

The energy blast escaped my hand of its own accord. It enveloped the two Shadows in a shimmering dome made of translucent energy, trapping them both inside.

They ceased their infantile brawl and glared at me.

"You only get out if you behave," I said.

Kirsi was rather amused.

Against my own instincts, I let the energy fizzle out.

Chaos exhaled hard through his nostrils. If looks could kill, Winter would soon be dead and buried. Chaos's words came out slurred with his lips bloodied and swollen. "You bedded the girl after I forbade it. I should disembowel you and make a necklace with your guts!"

Kirsi's jaw dropped.

"You're losing your powers old man," I told Chaos. "Maybe you have dementia or something. I'd rather sleep with a dust monster."

"I don't need powers for this. It's written all over both your faces. I see it and so does the Valkyrie."

Kirsi crunched up her face and nodded.

"And what is that to you?" I snapped. "You slept with my friend's mom. I can sleep with whoever I damn well please."

"Maybe your dipshit Romeo should have informed you about the dangers of consorting with a Shadow Warrior."

"Give it a rest. I knew enough and for your information that private moment was the only thing that saved us when Cerber trapped us both in an inverse energy reactor. We had no magic, just each other."

"If we're keeping score, I saved your life first when you were a baby," Chaos said.

Kirsi looked perplexed. "You did what?"

Chaos huffed. "Now killer Kirsi has curious questions."

Kirsi snarled. Winter yet remained silent, apparently having yielded the floor to me. I'd much rather he joined in. Talking to the Lord of the Black Hounds exhausted me.

"I thought your libido had been fed when you visited your wolf lover in his lair last week," Chaos said, rolling his eyes. "And *I'm* called the sex glutton."

Winter looked at the ground and rubbed his brow. I couldn't tell if Chaos and his bullshit about Emmet had hit a nerve.

"Enough with the fucking stalking," I said. "Get the fuck out of my head, Chaos, and out of my blood, too!"

"Said the girl who went to great trouble to summon me."

"You were summoned?" Winter said, finally speaking.

"Your soulmate didn't tell you, boyo? She lured me to help her face off with Cerber in the Dark Realm. She entered alone through the round."

So much for coming clean with Winter myself. Shit.

Chaos looked so pleased I was afraid a nonvoluntary blast would burn that grin right off his face. Winter remained stoic.

"How do I block you? How do I hit unfollow?" I told Chaos, seething. "I thought the third-eye vision was supposed to be used sparingly, how come you use it all the time like a porn addict when it comes to me? I am not living my life with you constantly watching. I'm not."

He smacked his lips together. "Are you done? Okay? You can relax, it's not as clear cut as that. I can sense where you are in the world, but I can't see you. Think of a radar map. I feel the radar blip, I can find you, but I can't see you. I won't know whether it's wolf season in your bed or Shadow season or guy you met at the bar after two Margaritas season."

"Dude, you suck," Kirsi said.

Winter punched his fist through the wall. "Enough! This is a classic *can't see the forest for the trees* scenario," he said. "We need to look at the damn forest. Horror has recovered enough of his power to allow Cerber passage to the basic world. They are the architects of the silver dust assaults, and what's next? They are going to breach the gates of the magic world. Our personal squabbles are meaningless. They're trees. We need to stop Cerber. We need to stop Horror. Every second that passes makes that harder."

Somber expressions overtook the room.

Winter's merciless eyes landed on Chaos. "When the Deep Down falls and Horror has absorbed all their magic, he will be coming for you next, Chaos."

Chaos muttered in what sounded like an ancient tongue. "Yes, you got me, old chum, I don't want to go out like a fucking tree."

The two Shadows nodded serenely at each other.

Am I hallucinating?

"Was that a friendly nod?" I said. "You two hate each other."

Chaos considered me with distaste. "Quite the opposite. Immortals have complicated relationships. They've been going on a while."

Kirsi sheathed her sword. "Works the same with the sisterhood. A lively sparring session speaks louder than words. It's honest."

Interesting. The struggle is real.

If they were all putting their differences aside to work on a common cause, I guess I had no choice but to do the same.

Winter fixed his gaze on me. "With Cerber on the loose, you'll be safer in the Deep Down. I'll drive you to a portal."

I nodded. My place was unlivable anyway. And I could finally get needed downtime to catch my breath and try to understand all that was happening.

Winter turned to Chaos. "You know what has to happen. Locate Cerber."

Chaos pulled a pale mask over his face. "The third eye cannot reach through the fog of the dark realm."

"The third eye will have to work twice as hard then," Winter said. "If for nothing else, to save your own skin."

We stepped out into the evening. The house sat alone atop a quiet hill. Winter rested his forehead on mine. Our energies mixed and mingled.

He opened the passenger door for me.

I hesitated. "What Chaos said about the enchanted rotunda..."

He banged the door shut. My heart thumped loudly as I waited for him to walk around the car, open his door and sit in the driver's seat next to me.

"Understand," he said. "I won't let Chaos get under my skin. I can't. Horror is the most lethal threat the living have ever faced. Cerber is his Grim Reaper." He sighed. "I'm not your keeper, Luna. Your life is yours. Yeah, I wish you would have come to me with the truth, but it's your truth."

Someone turn the A/C on. It just got hot in here.

"Right now," he said, "I'm just your driver."

Chapter 22

I THOUGHT I HAD seen some terrible things. I thought I knew what it was like to be flung in the middle of a horrific battle against your will, or to find yourself cornered by heinous forces dead set on destroying you, or to have the odds stacked against you *every last time*, but I hadn't seen the true face of evil until Cerber burst through my roof and choked me with his soul swallowing grip.

I curled into the car seat, knees to my chin.

Winter drove the car to the Deep Down gate at the enchanted waterfalls, the last portal in the area to remain open. The other portals had been sealed to heighten security due to the ongoing threat of silver dust.

Faion and I had gone through this gate earlier in the year. With any luck, Winter and I would get there before midnight.

"Was that the right exit?" Winter said after leaving the freeway.

I gave him a sideway glance. I wasn't sure where we stood but, for the first time, I trusted him completely. I knew he'd move heaven and earth to protect me, but I also knew the eventual showdown with Cerber would be mine and mine alone to fight.

"You always know where you're going," I said with a yawn.

"Am I boring you?" he said.

"I forgot what being bored was like. Sounds nice. My last 72 hours have been a series of hot messes, the immortal kind, with violence, threats and the grossest gory guts and green slobber..." I stopped as quite a different memory resurfaced. I tried not to grin. "And fucking Chaos, ugh."

"He is a lot," Winter said. "You know, it is what it is with him. We're going to need him, focus on that. Nobody else can locate Cerber. Our only chance might well be catching the necromancer by surprise."

I nodded. "I'm aware, but it's still the worst. And did you know Chaos can apparently move me around like a chess piece?"

He squeezed my hand and glanced at me. "How so?"

"He just ordered me to sit and I was impelled to sit. My free will gone. He said it's his blood in me and he can control it. I'm his human puppet. I swear, when this is over, I'm going to move all ten of his toes to his forehead. Let's see how charming women find him then."

Winter chuckled. "I very much doubt he can do that.

Don't let him fuck with your head. I know my former student—"

"And current bane of my existence," I said, finishing his sentence.

"He seems to have a soft spot for you. You're getting his good side."

"That's someone's good side?"

"As good as it gets," he said.

I pulled his hand into my lap. "Sad. Hey, what happened to you going crazy and telling me he's out to destroy me and all that?"

His face hardened. "Never saw him around you before, not like today."

I buried my face in my hands. "Confession time. He came to the Deep Down and I let him in. Don't yell. He neutralized the dust spell on Faion by absorbing it into his own body. And now that total asshat is going to swing that favor over my head like an axe for centuries to come."

Winter grimaced. "We are not going to let that happen."

We. We were a *we*–yet could never be a couple.

We fell silent. Distant lights of houses among citrus orchards and strawberry fields twinkled by. Winter pulled into a small gas station.

"Got to gas up," he said, twisting out of the car next to the pump.

I stepped out of the car, too, walking around to stretch my legs. The night was comfortably warm. A small gust blew in, carrying ocean scents.

If Helianna cornered me, I had no idea what I was going to say about the dust boxes I had given Grayson and Anya. I did know they better discover an antidote fast or the whole Double D would become a distant memory to any lucky enough to survive.

A woman stepped out from behind a parked truck. She was tall, dressed in black pants and a long cardigan and had a cream-colored turban on her head.

Her eyes shone bright in the dark. The way she stared was familiar. She was the same woman I had seen at Cyrus's gym, peering through the windows.

"Hey," I said.

She turned away. I followed her, building up to a brisk pace to keep up.

The woman crossed a street, walking through a red light.

"Please, wait a moment," I called after her. She stopped and turned back to me. In her gleaming eyes I saw hesitation.

"Sophie," I heard Winter's voice calling me.

The woman got spooked. She spun around and hurried off into the dark of the night, leaving no trace behind.

I returned to the car.

"Where did you go?" Winter said.

"There was a woman... I've seen her before. She was there at the gym, outside, before you got there that day, staring at me. Then just now, staring at me again, and both times she walked away. Poof!"

He arched an eyebrow. "*Poof?*"

A silver SUV rolled to a stop a few yards away. All four doors opened. Two women and a man stepped out, all three young and athletic.

The driver got out last. It was Cyrus McDonnell.

What the actual what?

Cyrus approached. The other shifters stayed back by the SUV, never removing their unblinking eyes from us.

"It took a lot of manpower to track you down," Cyrus said. "I committed every moving violation in the books to catch up with you."

Was the woman his spy?

I tried to look unimpressed. "Do you want a cookie or something?"

Cyrus flashed a smile. "We received our invite to present our case to the Board. You are to accompany us through the gate." He motioned Winter's old Civic. "At least, you're headed in the right direction."

Was I? I felt like I didn't know which way was up.

"You sent us into an ambush," Winter said, his voice as cold as ice.

Cyrus stepped to Winter with the grace of a predator cat. "Care to explain?"

"They were expecting us in Merida," Winter said. "We barely made it out."

Cyrus was entirely void of emotion. "You're telling me all my people died just to lure someone like you there?"

"Sophie would have never made it back had I not gone with her."

Okay, Winter, but please don't tell Cyrus how we got out.

Cyrus looked to the side. Menace teased at the corners of his mouth. "Are you saying that I would send little Miss Collinsworth into a deadly trap?"

Winter fixed his best psychotic glare on Cyrus. "Wouldn't be the first time you led a woman astray."

The other shifters moved in quick. Cyrus raised a hand. The shifters froze.

He matched Winter with a full-blown alpha glare. "There will be an apology now, for the greater good, or there will be blood."

I grabbed Winter's arm. His biceps were so tense they felt like cement. "Jonas, he never knew I would go. When he told me about the attack, he didn't even know there was a collection crew or that I was even the one that could help. And he certainly didn't know about you. Cyrus didn't kill his own people to set a trap. The pack only cares about the pack. He only wants to talk to Horpheus. Sending us to our death would be the worst move he could make. His intentions are primal and true. Emmet trusts him and I trust Emmet."

Winter's eyes glowed with violence. A wave of power glistened on his tense skin and washed over me, then ebbed. His face relaxed.

"It's your call," he said, looking into my eyes. "I'll let you make it." He turned and strode to the Civic.

"Prick," Cyrus said, quietly.

My hands itched with elemental energy. "Show some patience. He's not in a good mood." I breathed in. "You can follow us."

He clicked his heels together like a soldier. "Yes, ma'am."

I've been mocked by better.

Winter seemed unbothered when I got back to the car and we pulled out of the station. I stared at the dark road ahead, not knowing what to say. In the mirror, I saw the lights of Cyrus's SUV following at a safe distance.

How does one get four shapeshifters through the gate? Usually, each magic user entering the lower realm had to recite the magic script personally, but shifters never handled magic text very well, if at all. I would have to come up with a plan.

Without speaking a word, we finally reached the twin falls. The thundering crash of river water against the rocky, green plateau had a powerful, soothing effect, the best kind of magic—nature.

I led Cyrus and his bodyguards to the twenty-foot, diamond-shaped rock at the base of the river basin. Winter insisted going with us until we all had made it safely through the hidden gate behind the falling waters.

My hand found the rock face within the surrounding mist. I opened my mouth to pronounce the magic word when the ground shook underneath our feet and the portal opened.

"What's happening?" Winter said, wrapping his arm around me.

I shook my head. "Don't know."

The rock crackled with a sudden *whoosh*. A woman stepped through the gate: Celia Trice. Not far behind her, Penelope and then Gram did the same.

I thought I was hallucinating. Why would all three women who meant so much to me for different reasons come and greet me at the portal?

Gram looked straight at me and smiled. The benevolence in that smile almost broke down all the defenses I had built up on the way here.

"Penelope saw you would come through the falls," Gram said.

I fell into her arms and held on.

Celia stepped forward and stopped in front of Cyrus. "The West Coast Board of Supernatural Orders welcomes the San Diego shapeshifter pack leader to the Deep Down." She turned to Winter. "Magistrate, your presence is requested as well."

Did I hear that right?

Penelope stayed silent but regarded me with grave eyes. *Not good.*

The three women held hands as they faced the rock. Gram took my hand and pulled me forward, making us four strong.

Together we chanted the magic word, creating a chorus of fevered energy. "Succumb."

The falls shifted to envelop us all, completely cloaking our traveling party from the outside world.

We waited until all five guests had been sucked into the silver crease of light that cut through the center of the rock. Then we followed.

The rock crackled and slammed shut behind us.

We walked through silent corridors to the portal circle. We took the long path to Helianna's office in the *Magic Arts Hall*.

The Hall was chock full of people, some with their noses deep inside scrolls and documents, others gesticulating and talking out loud. The place fell quiet as our party entered the room. Those who had never left the Deep Down were stunned and unable to hide it. Shifters were like legends to many and like ghosts to others. Those who had traveled much, held more hostile expressions on their fixated mugs. A few whispered behind our backs.

A female dream-mancer waved us into Helianna's office. She handed Winter a visitor badge and scanned him with a handheld device.

"There is someone waiting for you, Magistrate," she said as she pointed to a door to the left. "Helianna will be with you shortly."

The door opened. I gasped. Magistrate Argos sat in a cushioned chair, legs crossed. His rough features tensed when Winter stepped into his view.

Argos was the last Immortal who should be allowed in the magic world. Did Helianna even know he had tried to bypass the wards of the Deep Down and install corrosive magic using Shaervas?

Without complaint, Winter stepped through the door and closed it.

What in all the worlds was going on?

Two guards approached Cyrus and his shifters, asking them to follow.

Cyrus fixed his eyes on me. "Will you join us?"

"I'm hardly an asset in such settings."

"It's the protocol," one of the guards said. "You need to go through the weapon scanners and sign an agreement of cooperation with security."

The shifters all followed the guards to the door. Cyrus suddenly turned his head around to salute me like I was a general. He assumed that light-on-his-feet feline stride, his shoulders swaying as he went. I knew he could trot like that for days and never tire.

Gram's hand landed gently on my shoulder. "Come this way, dear. I'm afraid our good friend Penelope had a new vision."

I followed Gram, Celia and Penelope to a small private hall.

"Why's the other magistrate here?" I asked as soon as we were alone.

"The Seventh Council has decided to be involved," Celia explained. "They negotiated a temporary truce so we can work together. Düsternis is in talks with Horpheus as we speak."

A shiver ran down my spine. "Düsternis is here, in the Deep Down?"

Celia shook her head. "No. They are meeting on neutral ground."

Thank Selene for small favors. I wasn't sure I'd be able to squash the desire to jump the Grand Magistrate if he crossed my path tonight.

Gram took my hand so I would sit next to her on the couch. "Darling, Penelope has something to tell you."

"Only us two," the seer said. "The words are for Luna's ears only."

Gram gave me an unhappy glance as she and Celia left the hall. That glance told me she knew I had a list of secrets I had kept from her.

I turned my attention to Penelope. "What's this? What words?"

Penelope placed her hands on my temples. "It is with a heavy heart that I speak these words, child. Only you, Luna Mae, can kill he who can't be killed. Fail to do so and all will be lost. The light will vanish from all worlds, darkness will swallow up young and old alike. Every soul will suffer in a state of suspended agony for eternity. The dark evil one must perish by your hand."

Yeah, better that Gram was not here for that. This night was becoming worse than the day that preceded it. Okay, I had to be the one to kill Cerber. I had suspected as much, but I was also fresh out of ideas as to how. Maybe Penelope could *see* some of those helpful words and share.

"Any words of advice?" I said. "Maybe a potion, or a cosmic cannon?"

She was not amused. "This is serious, you understand this, no?"

"Yes, I do, really. I make jokes when I am tired."

"Good. This you must figure out on your own." Penelope hesitated. "There is another matter. The Shadow Warrior, do you love him?"

Didn't see that one coming. "Can one love a shadow?" I said.

"This answer is not sufficient. It is, as you say, a cop out."

Bingo. "I don't have that kind of time, to love someone in that way, and even if I found the time, we could never be together. It's not in the cards."

Satisfaction sparked in her eyes. "*Bueno*, it's good you realize that. The Shadow is obsessed with you, so you have to hold the barriers up."

I've already dropped more than barriers.

"And if you ever forget this," she said, gazing into my eyes, "what such a *relación* would mean... you wouldn't just be forfeiting your life, you would be forfeiting his life too. Some things you bury so they won't bury you."

Chapter 23

THE MEETING TOOK PLACE in the colossal Great Hall that was usually reserved for grand occasions such as solstices, equinoxes, graduations and celebratory banquets of all kinds. I walked into the hall reluctantly, my every fiber telling me I didn't belong. I should be training right now, preparing for Cerber. As part of the collection crew though, my presence was required.

Every magic order and faction were represented around two stately long tables. At the far end of the hall a table on a raised platform awaited Horpheus, Helianna and the rest of the Board's high-ranking members. A handful of dignitaries milled about the room shaking hands, talking or standing alone deep in thought. Agatha, the Lunar Order's first, was chatting with Celia as they sat together at one of the long tables.

I scanned the room and spotted Winter next to a tall wind mage who used dynamic hand gestures while he talked. By

Winter's expression, I gathered he felt miserable. When did he tell me he had no patience for small talk? Ah, yes, nearly every time we were around people.

I made my way through a group of sorcerers. Winter spotted me. For a brief moment, a surge of relief rolled over his features. He caught himself and returned his bored professional mask back to his face.

He nodded a few more times, then excused himself. He came halfway across the hall to talk with me.

"Did Argos betray any of his devious intentions?" I asked.

"He's here on Düsternis's orders," he said. "The Seventh Council have decided that against this common enemy we must help each other."

"Took them long enough."

"It's a deception," Winter said. "Düsternis will never admit it, but he felt sidelined by Horror in favor of Cerber, his most hated enemy. His ego has never accepted it."

"Works for us, I guess."

"Argos will present the council's plan to the Board."

"This ought to be good."

All conversations ceased. All heads turned as one. Two troglodytes entered, tall and bulky, heavily armored like giant lobsters.

Behind them, Cyrus walked in. His posture was pristine and his gait fluid. His pants were black leather and his jacket burgundy velvet, a flattering ensemble that allowed enough freedom to run and pounce.

His three escorts trailed behind him, looking grim and hungry. Their smoldering eyes scanned the room for threats or targets or maybe both.

"All hail the plumed peacock," Winter said. "I need a brandy."

Cyrus took his seat at one of the tables. His escorts stood at a distance behind him. I took a better look at them. All three were dressed in *nouveau chic* biker apparel. One of the women appeared to be Native American with slick, dark hair that reached her waist. The other one was a pale redhead with a permanent frown fixed on her face. The guy had a powerful build, a strong jaw and tattooed forearms. His face expressed an unnerving indifference that felt like a warning to any who dared fuck with him.

The troglodytes were reluctant to sit. They had been assigned seats next to the shifters. One of the troglodytes leered at the standing shifters, while the other troglodyte pulled out a chair and bumped the powerful shifter. The pint of ale in his hand spilled all over the big shifter's shirt and jeans.

Before I knew it, knives had come out. Literally. The three shifters snarled as the troglodytes crouched behind their round bronze shields.

Why me? I had vouched for the shapeshifters and the first thing they did inside the Great Hall was start a fight.

Cyrus stood to glare at his fierce bodyguard. "Marlon, stand down."

The big shapeshifter's snarl stopped. His arms dropped to

his sides and his knife disappeared into a pocket. All three shifters seemed to shrink away when facing Cyrus. It was quite stunning to witness bloodthirsty shifters deferring to their Alpha.

"Forgive us, friends," Cyrus told the troglodytes. "We have not slept."

The troglodytes reluctantly sat down.

Cyrus discovered my eyes on him. He bowed slightly. I gave him one of my fakest smiles.

"The Great Chanter will join us presently," an official announced.

The few standing scurried to take their seats. I found mine next to Anya. Grayson sat on the other side of her. Winter walked back to his table where he was joined by Argos seconds later. I hadn't seen the bastard come in.

Horpheus, strode onto the raised platform followed by Helianna and five more high-ranking members of the Board.

"Please, rise for the Great Chanter and senior mage of the Board of Supernatural Orders," the official announced.

Everyone stood up, including me. It had been years since I had laid eyes on Horpheus. He always inspired great admiration and awe in me. He hadn't changed one bit. Same benevolent gray eyes, sharp features that hadn't softened with age, average height and long silver hair. He had the bearing of a man in his seventies but in truth he was well over 100.

He raised his right hand. "Friends, please sit," he said. "We are grateful you could all change your schedules to attend this assembly of supernatural beings on the West Coast."

Horpheus took his seat at the table, facing the room. Helianna sat to his right. A mage stood and began reading the protocol to be followed.

My mind drifted off. I couldn't shake the feeling we were wasting time. People would stand and talk and speculate and originate plans, but nothing would ultimately solve the problem.

A sudden urge grabbed me to spring up and tell everyone that we were talking in circles, and the only thing we had to do was to kill Cerber, the man who cannot be killed. Then I would tell them that I was the only person in the world who could make that happen and then...

And then, everyone would 1) laugh; 2) think I was crazy; or 3) throw me out of the hall.

The Chronomasters were called to the platform. Anya pushed her chair back and winked to me as she stood.

Grayson took the lead. "There's been a breakthrough," he said. "Thanks to one of our crew members, we had enough dust collected to keep all the chronochambers busy with multiple simultaneous experiments. And from this accelerated research we have made this profound discovery."

He placed a thin glass box on the table. A collective sigh rolled out from all assembled. A thin layer of silver dust sat at the bottom of the box.

Grayson revealed a second smaller box with a different

kind of dust—blue and coarser, like sand.

With a small scoop, he poured the blue dust into the silver dust box through a funnel spout. The silver dust reacted immediately, contracting and expanding, iridescent sparks sizzling inside the glass. A small puff explosion followed and then it was over. The silver faded away. All that was left was blue, non-reactive dust.

There was silence. Then the room erupted into applause. Spoons began to clink against teacups.

A few of us, including me, had tears welling in our eyes. They had done it! The Chronomasters had found the antidote to the killing dust. Everything Winter and I had endured at the massacre of Merida was worth it.

"Yes, there is cause to celebrate," Grayson said. "The progress is significant, but we are not home yet. We need more testing, more finessed trials to determine how to administer into living beings. The question of long-term side effects must be answered."

A member of the med crew stood up. "When will patients have it?"

"Soon," Grayson promised. "Relatively. When we're sure it's safe and we have produced a capable amount."

Winter stood. His face was hard to read.

"You can't use it," he said. "Not yet. Even if you finish your testing, we cannot reveal our greatest weapon to the enemy."

The room became deathly silent. Allowing immortal magistrates into the hall was one thing. Having them speak out of turn was another.

Argos rose. "Magistrate Winter is correct in his assessment," he said. He turned to Horpheus. "May I?"

Horpheus nodded. "Please."

Argos stepped onto the platform. "Esteemed leaders of the supernatural world," he started. His deep voice thundered through the hall. "On behalf of the Grand Magistrate Düsternis, I'm here to reveal the identity of the enemy behind the dust attacks on your people. As you must have surmised, we're dealing with the dark art of necromancy. We have every reason to believe the necromantic order is united in these assaults. All precautions must be taken to ensure our enemy will not learn our capabilities. If they think us vulnerable, that will be our advantage."

Murmuring and offended glares swept across the hall and with good reason. The Seventh Council wished to use us as bait.

"Hear me out," Argos went on. "In presenting a weakened defense, we can lure them to the Deep Down where your magic stands stronger. Unseal the portals, send your best people out in town, let the necromancers think your elite forces have left the Deep Down unguarded in order to defend San Diego."

"Excuse me, Magistrate," Helianna interrupted him. "How will *we* know when *they* plan to attack? Your plan is reckless. It may serve only to expedite our annihilation."

"We will be vigilant," Argos said. "Our elite forces will be at your disposal. And we have an embedded spy within the necromantic order."

A troglodyte stood up. "As most of you know, General Orsenio and his dishonorable miscreants defected to work with the necromancers. Not all of his men were of one mind. We have a patriot reporting back to us."

Argos glanced about the room, nodding. "The taste of victory will sweeten their blood and corrode their minds. Oh yes, they will come, and their own pride will lead them to ruin."

Of course, this scumbag would know that.

Horpheus opened his mouth. He spoke a few inaudible words.

All sound faded except the pounding of my own heart. My body felt light, weightless, like gravity had lost its hold.

I could hear myself blinking. My head swam up as my body was lifted and I now levitated near the ceiling. I could see everyone below, frozen in the positions they were in when time halted. In mid-sentence, leaning in, on their way to stand up, teacups inches from their lips.

Did the Chronomasters do this? No, both Grayson and Anya were frozen, glancing at each other.

An invisible dagger of dark power sliced through me.

I gasped, loudly.

Keep fighting destiny and you will lose everyone.

The voice was in my head and then it wasn't. It now belonged to a body and a face. Cerber. He hovered above the hall as I did. Two soul swallowers hovered behind him.

Winter, help! Someone... can't anyone see him?

"Your mongrel Shadow won't help you now," Cerber said greedily.

I started to panic. My lungs no longer took in oxygen.

"This has been predestined," he said. "You are mine."

Never.

"Are you going to kill me in a room full of people?"

He laughed. "The beings below us are there for a reason. They are lower life forms. They scurry about like cockroaches awaiting extermination while we higher beings go about our days."

He's not here. This isn't real.

His eyes became possessed. "I am Heka, I am Anu, the only one strong enough to protect you from the wrath of the third eye."

I stayed silent. What did the fiend want? He was no god, this much I knew, no matter what he said. Would he give me up to Horror or not? Maybe he wanted to be certain what I was before offering me to his master. Or maybe he just enjoyed toying with me.

"Another man, another promise," I said.

With a swoosh, he glided forward so we were eye to eye. "That tongue, I will enjoy ripping it from your mouth."

A dull ache ran through my core.

He's not here, he's not here.

"Surrender willingly. Save those you love," Cerber hissed.

"Good thing I'm smarter than that," I said, repeating Winter's words.

A viselike pressure gripped my head and squeezed. I saw stars as the pain consumed my skull. The agony blurred my vision. I fought to keep my eyes open, wrestled with my body not to vomit. I reached out to hold on to something but there was only air and an evil hologram.

A hidden force drilled into my skull, mainlining into my consciousness.

No! You're not violating me! You're not making me your third eye!

Energy trickled through me, raw, enraged, painful. I called it all to me, triggering it awake, oblivious to consequences. *Mine. All mine.*

I felt blood on my tongue. The smell of decay lingered in the air—the stench of death. My eyes burned. My body shook as I whimpered, but I kept gathering more force until I was nothing but a pulsating sphere of light.

Then I let it explode. Cerber's hologram shattered, fizzing back into primal particles. His face contorted into an ugly grimace.

"I'll meet you again on the battlefield." His voice was a distant echo.

The soul swallowers popped like bubbles and were gone.

I fell into a void. I felt limbless. I choked on my desire to scream.

Someone shook me. I blinked.

Anya's fearful face hovered above.

"Luna, are you okay, sweety?" she said.

My mouth felt full of dry cotton. "I feel sick. I need a moment."

I pushed my chair back and made a beeline for the exit, bumping into a few druids along the way.

In the long corridor, I had to support myself with the wall. I halted and slid down to the floor. I was shaken to my core. I buried my face in my hands. Cerber had drilled his way into my brain. He wanted a vantage point in which to watch the meeting. I hoped he didn't glean anything of importance in the few seconds he had to rummage through my brain.

"That bad, huh?"

Cyrus leaned back against the wall, crossing his arms.

I got back on my feet. "Not now," I told him.

He tried to say something, but I was already walking away. The lordly black panther had left the meeting he had wanted so much to attend just to follow me. Maybe Winter was right. Maybe Cyrus had sniffed out my unique essence and now hungered more answers.

Rounding a bend, I came upon Tam and Faion and my heart inflated. I'd never in my life been so happy to see two people.

"Who's that?" Tam said.

I turned. Cyrus had parked himself in front of an office door thirty feet behind me, hands in pockets.

"Never mind him," I said.

"But he's so pretty," Tam said innocently.

"He also comes with fangs the size of human thumbs," I warned. "He's the Higher Alpha of the San Diego pack."

"Oh my," Tam said.

"This gets better and better," Faion said.

"What does he shift into?" Tam said.

"A weasel," I snapped.

I stole a glance at Cyrus. He was amused. That's right, supersonic hearing, he'd probably heard everything.

"What happened in your meeting?" Faion said.

"I'm sure Celia will fill you in."

"Is it over?" Tam said.

I shook my head. "I felt indisposed, I'm going to lie down."

Faion folded his elbow around mine. "Want us to hang with you?"

A young man came running at us. A messenger.

"Luna Mae?" he said.

I nodded.

"This came in for you from the Ecuador portal. It bears the stamp of the local Board there."

I ripped open the envelope. In all capitals and in an exotic cursive script the message read:

TIME CAN BE STALLED...
-SHE WHO WATCHES YOU-

Chapter 24

I LAY ON A lounge chair on Winter's balcony in my shorts and tank top, letting the sun lull my senses, enjoying the temporary emptiness of my mind.

The ocean sparkled and glistened in the distance.

After three long days in the Deep Down, waiting for Cerber to make his move, I enjoyed this quiet morning under the sun.

The calm before the storm.

The necromancer hadn't tried again to possess my mind, but the creepy chill of that moment had never left me.

"He's here," Winter said, startling me.

I pulled my sunglasses down to glance up at him.

"Chaos?"

Winter sat down on the chair next to mine. "Damned if he hasn't kept his word. He's agreed to work on a plan to take down Cerber," he said, taking a sip from his Carlsberg beer bottle.

I sneered at him. "A plan? Let me guess, it ends with me in some horrible place fighting some horrible creatures."

We walked back inside. Chaos paced the living room, muttering. Bizarrely, he wore a turquoise t-shirt and print swim trunks.

"Hey, Chaos," I said. "Looks like you just knocked back some jello shots with the bros up in Venice Beach."

He considered his summery attire. "It's part of my cover."

I really didn't want to know what that meant.

"What do you have for us?" Winter said.

Chaos laid the map he carried on the table and unrolled it.

"The dark realm gates have been unlocked," he said. "The necromantic army and their legions of soul swallowers are unleashed."

Dread threw a party in my belly. For some reason, I'd thought we'd have more time. Time to strategize, to test the blue dust cure more thoroughly, time to go through all the worst-case-scenarios that might happen when I rode through the gates of Cerber's nightmarish realm.

"Where are they now?" Winter said.

Chaos pointed to a spot on the hand-drawn map. "Marching through the border between our two worlds. Unless they change course, in a day or two, they are going to clash with the Eternal Warriors that came out through the south equinoctial observatory."

Winter's eyes focused on the map. "They will change course. We can count on that. Cerber is no fool. He won't take on the Eternal army before he subjugates the world of magic and submits it to Horror."

"Horpheus and the Board," I said. "Do they know all this?"

"They have their sources," Winter said. "They'll know soon enough."

"Why not tip them off directly?"

Chaos opened his arms, exasperation lacing his features. "Why not give them my address and a golden dagger so they can slaughter me in my sleep, eh, honeybunch? My name can't be involved, not this time."

I held my tongue. What was it that Cerber had over him? Or was the possibility of a showdown with Horror the thing that had him so rattled?

"At least they have the counter dust," I said, pensively. "The researchers believe it can neutralize silver dust and reverse its effect on the victims, but it might also have a negative effect on the wielders of dark magic."

"Your fairy folk don't understand that their miracle cure is like putting a Band-Aid on a gunshot wound," Chaos said. "The war will never be won while Cerber yet breathes."

Winter clenched his jaw. "It's true. You are what Cerber wants now, even more than he wants dominion over the Deep Down. Yielding your power to Horror would immediately make him a thousand times stronger."

Yeah, I was the bait alright. But also the hook.

Chaos scooped up some dried nuts from a crystal bowl

and popped them into his mouth. "Cerber still serves Horror. He takes his directives straight from the Eternal madman, but..." He stopped to toss more nuts in his mouth.

He chewed eagerly and loudly.

"Chaos!" I scolded him. "Don't talk when you eat."

"Right. Communications between Cerber and Horror are scarce and coded. Horror is under strict monitoring. He has to avoid suspicion. There's a good chance Cerber hasn't sent back any meaningful intel yet."

Winter creased his brow. "Cerber may be the only one who knows the true nature of Luna's etheric essence."

"Or that two Shadow Warriors are guiding her," Chaos added.

Huh. I'd never thought of it that way before.

"So," I said, unsure, "if Cerber is eliminated before reaching out to Horror, this whole mess could end. What about the part where he can't be killed?"

Winter pinched my nose with his knuckles. "We'll see how he fares against two shadows."

Chaos snorted. "Brother, he will never face us in this world. He'll try to lure us to the dark realm where his power reigns supreme."

Winter shrugged. "We'll cross that bridge when we come to it."

"This isn't a job for shadows," I said.

They stared at me. I had succeeded at shutting them up.

There was an innocence in them that I had never seen

before. "Listen, fellas, I appreciate your courage, I really do, but this is a one-woman job. I have to be the one to do it," I said, looking to Winter. "Alone."

Chaos looked stymied. "She believes what she's saying."

"Penelope's prophecy was clear," I said, "and that peculiar woman has never once been wrong. I must kill he who can't be killed, or all will be lost."

"Hogwash," Chaos said.

I blocked the peanut bowl as he tried to take another handful. "You've held a grudge against Penelope ever since she told me it was you who had given me to Winter."

"The woman doesn't merit a grudge," he said, defeated.

"It doesn't matter what Penelope merits or doesn't merit. This is my fight and it's been a long time coming. I think you both know that."

"Out of the question," Chaos said. "No."

"No?"

"You'll be the bait. That's where it ends," he insisted.

"This is my destiny. I'm not going to run from it." I looked to Winter. "Mist riders never turn away, isn't that what you keep telling me?"

His eyes sparked and raged. "You're asking me to let you walk into the most savage of duels on your own and, basically, weaponless. There is only one way that can end, Luna. It will be *you* or *him*."

"If he survives, I'll be toast anyway. I'd rather die than end up as Horror's slave. I have to give it a try, Jonas. If I fail, you two can jump right in and finish Cerber. The world still wins. What have I been training for anyway?"

"I can't let you die," he said.

Isn't he sweet? I feel the same way about him.

"Sooner or later, you have to believe in someone besides yourself. Both of you. Trust your girl. I can do this. I will do this."

"For fuck's sake, this is like watching *Sophie's Choice*," Chaos snarled. "And we're fresh out of salted nuts."

I ignored him. "I'm going to face Cerber," I said. "That's a fact, but I will need a ton of help to make it happen."

Winter closed whatever gap there was between us. His eyes were darkened by a new determination.

"Kirsi and I will make sure the Immortal convoy creates a distraction when Cerber appears to claim you," he said. "Chaos will teleport you to wherever Cerber flees, away from witnesses. This fight can't happen in front of human eyes, basic or magic."

That was it then. He was giving me his blessing.

He disappeared into his bedroom.

We stood there, waiting for him to come back, every second feeling like an eternity. Chaos jangled the keys in his swim trunks.

Winter returned holding a sheathed sword.

"An Italian sorcerer awarded me this in the twelfth century," he said as he set it in my hands. "A magic infused blade won't help a great deal against Cerber on his own turf, but it'll provide the best training."

I slid the sword from its sheath and stared at the shimmering blade. Magic nipped at my fingers when I touched the steel. It was by far the heaviest sword I had ever held.

"Horror's dagger that Cerber possesses, is it real?" I said.

"Yes," Chaos said coldly. "To follow him through space, I'll have to physically be in the same plane of existence as Cerber."

At great risk, I knew. We all would face that risk. *Death.* That's not usually on the Immortal dance card.

Chaos put both his hands on my shoulders. "Once in the dark realm, don't look him in the eye, don't get dragged into his game of supremacy. Just wait for the right moment to kill him. Buy time any way you can."

Chaos was sincerely solemn. Not a good sign.

"Oh, I almost forgot," I said. I grabbed my purse and found the cryptic note inside. "This was delivered to me outside the Great Hall. I think it's from the woman I caught watching me a couple of times."

Winter read it and then handed it to Chaos.

Chaos went completely pale as he read.

"Does it mean anything to you?" I said, noticing his reaction.

He took a long breath. "More hogwash, I suspect," he said. "Gotta run, Eternal people. There's a tide shift due at Pacific Beach and the waves are going to be heavy today. I'm amped to get my new board wet."

And like that, he was gone.

I turned to Winter. "Did you see his face when he read the note? I mean, does he even surf? That was just odd."

Winter shrugged. "I don't speak Chaos. C'mon, you need sword training."

EVERYTHING HURT IN A dull, persisting way, my whole body aching down to the last muscle, bone and ligament.

Winter didn't fool around when it came to training. His blade had given me the beating of a lifetime but had also taught me how to stay on my feet under relentless assault.

I closed the bathroom door and stripped down quickly. A few bruises on my hips, a result of me falling multiple times, were already healing.

It'd been a long time since I luxuriated in a lazy, revitalizing bath. I let the hot water run as I threw some magnesium salts and lavender oil in the bath water to create a fragrant steam.

I lit two vanilla scented candles and turned off the light. Winter had all the pampering necessities. I didn't wait for the water to fill the tub before I stepped in. I closed my eyes as I soaked myself in the frothy water, trying to reconcile myself with the idea that sometime soon my frail human body would have to fight a demon from a place worse than hell to death.

The hot water was up to my neck now. I turned off the tap.

There was a moment of total silence in my soul, a feeling of melancholy that stemmed from places inside I'd rather not explore. I taught myself long ago not to visit those damaged places in my mind where all thoughts led to self-pity about what broke in me after I lost my mother.

The door opened a crack. "May I come in?" Winter said.

My heart skipped a few beats. "Ah, sure."

He stepped in the bathroom and leaned against the doorframe. Seeing his body silhouetted against the electric light from the hallway was magnificent.

His skin, his power and grace possessed all my senses. Winter was *beautiful*. Maybe that's not the word to use for a beefy man, but if you haven't been in that tub and stared upon that man, you wouldn't understand.

His piercing blue eyes offset everything with an intense intimacy.

"If I hadn't agreed to your insane plan, you'd have run off and done it without me, wouldn't you?"

I smiled. "Everything is much better with you."

My phone buzzed.

"Can you get it for me?" I asked him.

He moved to the sink and picked up the phone. "It's the wolf," he said, arching his eyebrows. "Do you want to answer?"

I shook my head. "Nah. He'll leave a message. Nothing happened between us, you know. Ever. Plus, Cyrus warned me to stay clear of Emmet."

"He did what?"

I closed my eyes. "He thinks I'm a bad influence."

His hand touched my shoulder. My fierce Immortal was on his knees, crouching next to the tub. "If that pompous predator even so much as looks at you wrong, I'll mount his head on my wall."

I laughed. "What a big bad brute you are, Jonas Sandell."

He reached over and grabbed the shampoo bottle.

I stared at him. "Really? You're going to shampoo my hair?"

"Just close your eyes and relax."

"Try not to get soap in my eyes."

"Yes, ma'am," he said, turning the showerhead on to wet my hair.

I lay back and relaxed my shoulders, my eyes half-shut. His hands lathered my hair slowly, gently massaging my scalp.

May this moment last forever.

I faded away into total bliss. Later, when he finished rinsing the soap off my hair, he leaned in and kissed my wet neck, and then he bit down on my shoulder softly. I shifted my weight a little but kept my eyes shut, terrified of my own body's responses.

"Promise me you'll return to me," he whispered.

"I promise I'll try and try," I said, moaning involuntarily.

His fingers traced my collarbone and then covered my throat before they found the back of my neck, pulling my face to his. My heart erupted in a million different directions.

"I'm serious, Luna. If during the fight you think Cerber has every advantage, I want you to find a way out of there."

"And all the world can go to hell?"

"The world is already hell without you," he said.

Chapter 25

Nightfall had settled over the streets of San Diego when Chaos teleported me right to the heart of the Astral Square in the Deep Down. The place had been picked because of its proximity to the Carlsbad portal where Cerber's forces were headed and also because it offered an abundance of hiding spots.

The plan was to hold until the necromantic army rushed through the square on their way to the Central Chamber where the master orb was kept. Possession of the orb was crucial to accessing the ferocious whirlpool of energy that dwelled in the Deep Down.

I stood on top of the library building, a hundred yards from Astral Square. Chaos stood next to me, looking even grimmer than usual.

"I must go," he said. "If Cerber senses my essence, he might not risk showing up. I'll wait for your signal."

My signal would probably end up being my blood

curdling fear. That's what Chaos would sense.

"Till then," I said.

The Shadow spun away into a whirlwind of vanishing blue smoke.

I wasn't supposed to be here. I wasn't a warrior nor was I chosen by my Order to function as a second line defender. To the Deep Down, I was still an undertrained lunar witch.

Winter climbed up to the roof like a huge spider. He was dressed in black. A six-foot-two wall of muscle, man and Shadow.

I barely quelled my desire to fall into his arms.

"Look," he said, pointing down at the square. "The sorcerers are positioned along the path leading to the portal. The troglodytes are right behind them ready to slaughter whoever breaks through the sorcerers' interlaced shields. Across the street from us, the druids and the mages lie in wait. Your Lunar Order is behind the clock tower along with sister orders. If you see over there, three blocks out, the Chronomasters are waiting, surrounded by a warrior squad. The Immortal elite forces are hiding inside the little bakery shops. And right there, in the middle of the square, the shapeshifters are crouching behind the large marble fountain, hidden by a veil of darkness."

I had been trying to act cool, but now I was floating. The countdown had begun. And when all factions failed to repel Cerber, it would be up to me to save the Deep Down and then end his life force.

Winter stared into my eyes. "No matter what happens down there, no matter what you see or hear, you cannot join the battle. You can't reveal yourself or your powers, do you understand?"

"Yes," I said, my lips as stiff as the rest of me.

He turned to go, changed his mind, grabbed me with one hand behind my neck, another on my hips, and kissed me. "Remember to remain in one piece," he said, then leaped into the dark streets below.

I touched my mouth with the back of my hand to feel his lips there. If it was my final kiss in this life, I wanted to savor it.

A shrieking howl tore through the quiet of the night, followed by the rising echoes of an approaching stampede. I felt a rolling energy flowing beneath me across the square and the buildings.

Not yet, not yet.

Breathless minutes ticked by. A lone man emerged on the portal path. I crouched and looked through the night vision goggles.

Average build, balding, wearing a long white tunic—a soul swallower. More soul swallowers crept forth behind him, then in one breath a whole line of them appeared, then another line and another line.

Legions of dust monsters trotted along, ugly, green, slobbery.

Nobody move yet, nobody move.

Finally, the necromancers strode in, dark magic flaring about their cloaked bodies.

I didn't see Cerber among them, but I saw something else. Down in the square, a majestic white wolf crouched next to a pack of gray wolves.

Emmet.

Why was he here? Had he even fought before?

Maybe that's what he tried to tell me when he called the other night.

Black smoke breached the portal, slithering its way along the ground.

Wait, wait.

The necromantic procession came to a halt. The soul swallowers drew small canisters from underneath their tunics. They unscrewed the lids on the canisters and started spreading silver dust.

Mad cackling rolled through the square.

One more beat... and... Now!

Mages, witches and sorcerers sprang forward, deluging the soul swallowers in blue dust.

The uglies screeched, clawing at their throats as they gagged.

Dark magic erupted from the necromancers like long, suffocating tentacles. All magic factions joined powers to fight off the dark energy.

The ground shook as the shapeshifters flew out of hiding in animal form and pounced on the necromantic army with guttural howls, slashing teeth and razor-sharp fangs. The Immortal elite forces broke through the shop doors in heavy black armor swinging wide-blade swords. Before I remembered to breathe, the grounds below me had turned into a battlefield.

I stayed low and spied the fight below for signs of Winter, my heart in my mouth. It was impossible to spot any faces in the heat of the titanic combat.

Then I saw him, blurring past a group of dust monsters, cutting down the whole lot with a single swipe of his sword before he crashed shoulder first into two necromancers.

Dark magic spread out and knocked Winter back. It didn't faze him. He bounced back to his feet and raised his hand to them. The necromancers went down, grabbing their throats with both hands.

His sword came down next, severing one necro head and then the other.

A horde of soul swallowers attacked him. Winter spun like a dervish, hacking them down until they became a ring of blood-drenched corpses surrounding him. Kirsi sprang to his side. Blood covered her face. They took off into the battle and I again lost sight of them.

Fallen bodies from both sides were littered everywhere. I had no idea who had the upper hand.

Surging lights sparked above the square as energy bolts were hurled left and right. A man broke away from the fight and climbed up the marble fountain. It was Grayson. He held something in his hand and raised it above his head. I focused my goggles on him. He had a timestop watch. He would try to use the water energy to fuel it, so he could manipulate time.

I felt the malicious presence before I saw him. Cerber flew in like a nightmarish vulture and landed on the fountain next to Grayson.

My body went cold, my limbs numbed. I held my hands over my mouth to stifle a scream. With blinding speed, Cerber drove a dagger deep into the Chronomaster's eye. Grayson's sandy blond head fell back as the light extinguished from his face. His lifeless body rolled into the fountain water.

An inhuman wail cut above the clanging and the roaring of the battle, sharp like an animal being hit by a car. Anya sprinted across the square to get to Grayson, screaming the whole way.

Cerber's eyes tracked her as she ran. Rage and agony built to a roaring crescendo inside my soul. I shot up and screamed out: "Changer of faces!"

Cerber's head rotated swiftly in my direction like it was mounted on a swivel.

That's right, here I am, you bastard!

He flew to the roof and landed inches from me. The golden dagger in his hand was already streaked with red.

"We meet again, little bitch," he said with a wide grin. His teeth were small and sharp. It looked like there were twice as many as the usual thirty-two in his mouth.

I gathered energy and motioned him to come. He raised the dagger as he strode forward.

Chaos materialized behind me. He tugged me to his chest and spun, tendrils of smoke swallowing us up a fraction of a second before Cerber slashed through me with the dagger.

Cerber swore in various tongues. Even from inside the smoke, I could hear his venomous voice. I could see him too, his eyes brimming with malice, his face blistering and puffing up like it was about to change age.

Chaos had kept us suspended inside the blue smoke, caught in a place between places. Through a thin veil of vapor, we watched the battle, unseen and undetected by those who fought in it.

A unit of five Immortals with Argos in the lead climbed onto the roof. Cerber tried to shoot up and away, but two Immortals intercepted him, trapping his neck between their blades.

Cerber's face snapped back into place.

Argos stepped forward, his sword drawn. "On behalf of the Grand Magistrate, I place you under arrest for having breached the gates of the magical world," he said.

Argos drove his blade clean through Cerber's stomach.

Cerber winced.

"This blade has been forged with sterling silver, manganese and bonshek. It will keep the wounds open until Düsternis determines a way to terminate you permanently."

Argos stabbed Cerber again and again. His face was gleaming with the sinister grin of a man used to torturing. Blood spurted out from the necromancer's mouth and nose. Then Argos cawed unnaturally.

The doomed Immortal's hands dropped the sword and grabbed onto the golden dagger protruding from his chest.

A tall woman climbed onto the roof.

It's she who watches me!

Cerber grabbed the twin blades on his neck with both hands. The blades turned into liquid metal. The golden dagger flew back into Cerber's hands. Argos dropped to his knees, blood spurting from his body like his pipes had burst.

The four remaining Immortals lunged at Cerber. He enveloped them in a wave of black smoke that sent them flying off the roof.

The woman pointed her right index finger at Cerber. "Necromancer, you will never stop Time!"

Cerber dove at the woman, clutched her in a savage headlock and flew upward with her until they were sucked into a different dimension.

Argos's body collapsed forward, his life force extinguished.

I shivered. The dagger was real. It could end immortal lives. I was weaponless and in no way a match against Cerber. What if Penelope was wrong? What if this time she had misread her visions?

The Immortal plan had failed. I had doubted it from the

start, but wouldn't it have been nice if they had killed the bastard or thrown him in an endless loop of agony like Argos had promised?

The world spun until my feet landed on the ground. Chaos popped right next to me on the roof.

His eyes were haunted. "It's time," he said. "I have him."

Pain hit me everywhere inside at once. All I wanted was to curl into a fetal position and cry. I wanted it all to have been a dream.

The battle raged, good people were dying everywhere. My teary eyes glared into the black Shadow's weary eyes. "Take me to him. I'm ready."

Chaos scooped me up with one arm. The smoke came in angry swirls and carried us off the roof to the arid no man's land with the fine golden sand and the line of dry bluffs I had visited here once before via the enchanted rotunda.

The Dark Realm.

Strange that it's always sunny here.

The smoke still protected us. I saw Cerber and the woman silhouetted against the hot sun like desert mirages. The woman's face was bloodied. Cerber yanked the turban off her head. A cascade of slick white hair swirled about her face and down onto her shoulders. Cerber slapped her hard twice on both cheeks. My blood boiled.

"Leave us," I told Chaos. "I have homework."

Chaos flared his nostrils. "I will set wards at all nearby exits."

He hesitated. "You will be trapped in his world with him."

"Find Winter," I said.

When the smoke evaporated and Chaos with it, the energy shift nudged me forward. I nearly lost my balance.

Not the most graceful entrance.

Cerber loosened his grip on the woman. His eyes had found me.

The golden dagger was sheathed at his waist. His jacket had multiple holes where Argos had stabbed him, but the Changer of Faces was already healed in his kingdom.

"How about you pick someone your own size?" I yelled.

Cerber looked around, uncomprehending. "Who could you mean? All I see is two little bugs who need to be squashed."

"All your uglies are gone, huh?" I said, walking toward him. "Fell into an obvious trap even an absolute novice could have smelled out."

The woman's eyes sought refuge in my eyes. She oozed with terror.

Cerber grinned. "Well, you're a novice who just fell into my trap."

"I'm right where I want to be," I said.

"I love it when my food is delivered," he said. "Especially when..."

He didn't get to finish that sentence. Fast as lightning, I shot a handful of blue dust into his face and ran away as fast as my legs could take me.

Behind me, the necromancer moaned, then went silent.

He must be choking on the blue dust.

I ran and ran until I couldn't feel my legs anymore.

"Watch out," the woman cried. Her voice reached me as if from a dream.

I twisted around. Cerber kneeled and slammed his fists on the sand, sending an incredible wave of energy my way.

The force hit me while I was preparing a shield. I went airborne and then crashed against a boulder so hard bones cracked. My side was gashed, and I coughed up a mouthful of blood. I tried to get up, but my ribs were cracked and moving felt like smashing into a wall of pain.

The necromancer hit me with a second power wave. This one set my insides on fire like I was hit with a megaton of voltage. I screamed. My flesh smelled like burnt hair and chargrilled pork.

I stayed down, shaking.

Penelope really needs a new job.

Cerber raged across the field to join me.

My heartbeat thundered as he approached. I had no feeling in my extremities. So much necromantic magic was hard for any being to recover from, even a mist rider.

I looked at the sky and squinted at the sun. A single tear ran down my cheek.

The necromancer's gaze locked on me as he lifted me by the hair. An earsplitting growl ripped from his throat. "You'll never again be free!"

I gathered every last vestige of strength in me. I finally allowed the mist to come to me, spilling out of my hands in thick clumps. Cerber turned pale and went for my throat with fingers oozing of black smoke. Too late. I snatched the golden dagger from his waist and rammed it into his heart.

Cerber shrieked. His hands shook as he tried to grip Horror's dagger and remove it from his chest. His fingers could never quite land.

I chuckled painfully. "Your second trap, letting you think you were easily beating me. The only way I could get you close enough with your guard down."

The mist enveloped my mangled body to begin the healing.

I removed the pouch from my pocket with the last grains of blue dust.

"Your own medicine, General," I said. "How do you like it?"

Cerber lay on his back. His breathing was labored. "What are you?" he whispered. "You can't be his child."

I leaned in. "Whose child?"

The necromancer's body went cold and shivered. His voice leaked out raspy and low. "He will avenge me."

A final shudder finished him. Cerber's eyes closed. He was no more.

"It wasn't you he was after."

I turned. The white-haired woman watched me with glassy eyes.

Standing up took effort. "How do you mean?"

The woman towered over me. "It was me he wanted. I was sent to find you and relay a message. Cerber didn't want that message delivered or me to go on breathing. He knew I'd never rest until I put it in your hands, but I couldn't risk talking to you while he watched you. He tried to kidnap you so I'd fall into his deadly trap."

I felt like a fool. Cerber had no idea what I was until the moment I stepped into the rotunda. I had revealed my nature to him and now I would never know if Cerber had notified Horror of his discovery.

The woman lowered her eyes. "My time is running out. I hold the key to Horror's defeat."

"How do I defeat Horror?" I blurted out, eagerly.

She considered me with sad eyes. "You're not yet ready, Luna Mae."

The woman who watches reached inside her pocket and handed me the note that had caused so many deaths.

"My task has been achieved," she said. "It's from your mother."

My world stopped. Thin breaths escaped my paralyzed lungs. My stomach ached like I would throw up. "It's from my mother?" I repeated.

The woman raised her eyebrows. "The time will come, when the mother of your birth will find you."

She walked away, slowly, yet her body quickly blended into the horizon and faded from sight.

I never even thought to ask her name.
I unfolded the note and read it out loud:

You are of time and of mine, daughter of time. When your destiny arrives, I will soon follow.

When Winter broke through the sky and descended slowly, the tears finally came and I was four again and it was a sunshine world, a world of bright dreams and smiles that ran ear-to-ear and arms, warm arms that knew me and wrapped me up in warmth that felt like forever.

Winter found me like that and try as he might, the tears kept flowing.

Chapter 26

TWO DAYS LATER

WINTER SAT ON A jagged rock by the edge of the lake, skipping pebbles. His face was hard to read, but today he promised he would finally give me answers.

I had struggled to come to terms with the insanity of the night I faced Cerber in the Dark Realm. The soul swallowers and the slobber monsters had turned to dust when I killed their master and the remaining necromancers fled, but the devastating toll inflicted upon the magic factions had been profound. The med crews and the healers had worked a thousand miracles, but despite their best efforts nearly two hundred souls were lost.

We were all heartened to hear the blue dust had been effective in resuscitating the silver dust victims. Unfortunately, it turned out my mother had not been a silver dust victim and she had not awakened.

"They died right here, you know," Winter said.

I pricked up my ears waiting to hear more.

"Helen and the baby. The cab they were taking was struck by another car and veered into the lake. All three drowned. Helen, my bright boy Christian and the cab driver, her name was Susan."

The weight I felt on my chest was crushing. Everything was pushing up into my throat. It was the saddest story I had ever heard. I closed my eyes, breathed deeply to calm down and tried not to steal the attention.

"I thought you were in London," I said.

His eyes were on the lake. "We were. I brought them out here when Christian was ready for travel. We were relocating to San Diego so I could resume my duties as Chief Magistrate. For years, I thought that decision had killed them."

"It didn't," I said. "Get that thought out of your mind."

"I come here to feel close to them. Conceiving the child was not the plan, but when I first held Christian in my arms, I wanted nothing more."

I could not imagine the anguish in his heart, the helplessness, the emptiness of arms robbed of a child. I touched his sad face.

Winter took my hand and kissed it.

"Enough," he said. "For what I'm about to say, you should sit."

"Alright," I said, sitting on the rock beside him.

"Chaos is your half-brother."

Wow, he just said it like that. I wasn't prepared.

"You and Chaos share a father," he went on. "Your mother took you to Chaos and asked for his help. She feared for your life once others had discovered what you were. Then Chaos turned to me, his mentor and old friend. He believed you'd be safer if I were the one who found you a home."

I struggled to process the colossal revelations he had dumped on me.

"My father is Immortal?" I said, finally making sense of things.

"Indeed."

"Who is my father? Or my mother for that matter?"

"I don't know. Chaos never betrayed that information. He bound me with the oath of Shadows never to seek out your parents' identity."

"Explains his glee at destroying the Sacred Vault archives," I pondered out loud.

Winter turned to me. "Only he can answer that question."

"Except he has conveniently disappeared—again. I'm really tired of figuring out ways to smoke him out."

"Or you could just go to him."

I eyed him suspiciously. "Do you know where he is?"

"No, but you do."

Huh?

"How do you think he's able to find you?"

"The third-eye vision."

He shook his head.

"How then?"

"He bound you to him through blood even before he brought you to me. You already had a blood connection when Chaos gave you his blood to heal. He can feel your etheric essence at all times and if you honed your mist rider skills, that would become a two-way channel."

I knew it!

"Wait, then why did he have to orchestrate the whole metamorphic night just to force you to reveal me?"

"My prime responsibility once I became your guardian was to keep you hidden from Chaos for as long as I could. His volatile nature and his flimsy grasp on self-control were always a concern. So I cloaked your etheric essence and shielded your blood before I placed you with a family."

"But Chaos easily duped you into revealing me anyway."

There was hesitation in his eyes.

"Spit it out," I said.

"I had overreacted in keeping him from you. Chaos was in love with your mother. He vowed to her he would keep you safe. I didn't think him capable of honoring a vow, but that vow he has honored."

"Are you telling me Chaos fell in love with his father's wife?"

Winter nodded. "He already loved her before she married your father. That's all he would say. I think Chaos loves her still."

Right. So his concern wasn't for me. He hadn't become my protector out of brotherly love. It was all for my mother, whoever and wherever she may be.

Chaos eternally in love with one woman? That may have been the most shocking news of all. It did explain a lot. *Yes, now I see.* When he read that first message from the white-haired woman, he knew it was connected to my mother. No wonder he suddenly became a surfer and escaped Winter's condo like his ass was on fire.

"Is my mother a mist rider? Who exactly is she protecting me from?"

"Luna, I don't know. And it wouldn't be mine to tell you."

That was it. I ran out of questions, or I ran out of the energy needed to learn more. I mean, who cared what would happen when/if Horror found out Chaos was my big brother, the man he hated the most? I didn't. In fact, I'd even stopped caring what would happen with Winter.

I leave that to destiny.

"Will you go back to Stockholm?" he said.

"I don't know."

Neither of us wanted to be the next person to speak.

"I think you should," he said.

Another blow to my heart, even though I knew he was right.

"Fine, I'll go back to Stockholm," I said.

"I'm not the enemy, Luna."

"What are you then?"

He had no answer for that. The only one I really needed.

"Will your watchers still get their kicks watching me dress and undress? Or picking my nose or whatever?"

"They won't," he said. "They never did that."

"Oh," I said. "Even they have abandoned me."

He was unsure how to respond. "Luna…"

I punched his ribs. "I'm fine, you idiot. I'm messing with you."

"There will be no watchers. You're free to live your life."

Once upon a time that would have been enough.

"You say that like it's a good thing."

I wanted to fall into his arms, lay my head on his chest and listen to his heart beating out an eternal rhythm. Instead, we stared out at the quiet lake waters, side-by-side, until it was time for us to leave and wander back to our separate lives.

About the Author

Stella Fitzsimons was born in Athens, Greece, and lives in Southern California with her husband and two sons. After studying economics and language arts she went on to teach both Mathematics and English before launching *Stella's Literary Bistro*, a bilingual literary journal. Her works include: *Luna, Winter, Silver Dust, Shadow Fall, Moonlight Mist* and *The Last Rider.*